The Talent

Stories of Authors and Artists

The Talent

Stories of Authors and Artists

Missouri Review Books

Edited by Kristine Somerville and Speer Morgan

Published by Missouri Review Books
455 McReynolds Hall, University of Missouri
Columbia, Missouri 65211

Missouri Review Books is published by the *Missouri Review* through the College of Arts & Science of the University of Missouri, with private contributions.

The Talent: Stories of Authors and Artists

ISBN: 978-1-945829-70-3 (print)
ISBN: 978-1-945829-71-0 (digital)

Library of Congress Control Number: 2023917901

www.missourireview.com

Cover Image: *Beauty Sleep*, Angelica Paez, 2014

Cover design by Jane Raese of Raese Design, Boulder, Colorado.
Interior design by Scott McCullough.

Special thanks to Associate Editor Evelyn Somers who edited the stories when they first appeared in the *Missouri Review.*

I am interested in art as a means of living a life;
not as a means of making a living.

Robert Henri

Table of Contents

Foreword ix

Ursula and Will / *Catherine Gammon* 1

Door to Everything / *Frank Montesonti* 15

Swarm / *Lauren Acampora* 25

You're Starting to Get a Reputation / *Therese Eiben* 45

The Prodigal Daughter / *M.G. Stephens* 59

Oonark/ *Elizabeth Altomonte* 71

A Quiet Pilgramage to Every Last Ruined Saint / *Gabrielle Hovendon* 83

The Pickers / *Ernest J. Finney* 97

Kristin's Uncle Otto / *Kerry Hardie* 117

Banned / *Laura Venita Green* 135

Babette Has Gone Missing / *Becky Mandelbaum* 159

Contributors' Notes 179

The Talent Teacher

In biographies of American artists of the late nineteenth and early twentieth centuries, Robert Henri's name appears often. While he was known as cofounder of the Ashcan School of urban realism and an exceptional painter of portraits, he was even more acclaimed as America's finest art teacher. George Bellows, Edward Hopper, John Sloan, and Rockwell Kent, among others, were devoted pupils. To critics they recalled that he guided not only their art but also their lives by encouraging them to live richly in the world.

Henri's teaching career began in 1891 at the Philadelphia School of Design for Women, where he taught drawing and composition classes. He loved teaching from the start. His approach was to take student work seriously and make students believe that art was a necessary and fundamental part of their lives. He taught that the only law of artistic composition was to tell a story; beyond that there were no set rules.

His curriculum consisted of having students produce pencil and charcoal renderings of Greek and Roman figures, a traditional approach based on his training at the famed Parisian schools the Académie Julian and the École des Beaux-Arts. A tall, rangy, dynamic figure, he especially impressed young female students, who found his lectures hypnotic and the intensity of his charm irresistible. While they worked at their easels, the walls and their smocks covered in paint, the smell of turpentine in the air, he regaled them with stories of his days in Paris, from which he had returned in 1890. He'd lived with four fellow Americans, crammed into a fifth-floor garret with a stove, water basin, pitcher, and coal-burning fireplace, subsisting on horsemeat and rice, sometimes soup.

He'd loved the rigors of his schedule at the Julian. At seven am, he'd dash across the Seine, grab a café au lait at his favorite creamery, and then fight his way into the crowded studio of easels for a good view of that day's model as she disrobed in the sunlight from the skylight windows. During their lunch break, students would burst into song, lift weights, box, and gossip. A blue haze of cigarette smoke hung over the classroom.

To prepare for his entrance exams at the Beaux-Arts, he spent evenings studying at the National Library poring over books on the art of Greece, Rome, and other ancient cultures. Each year more than four hundred candidates sat for the four-day exam for eighty openings. It took Henri two tries to gain entrance, but after one year of study at the famed art school, he felt torn between the desire to paint spontaneously and the formal classroom approach. Still, he carried on the school's tradition of learning to draw by copying classical statuary and recreated the messy yet productive ambience of the Parisian classroom.

Henri would go on to teach at the New York School of Art, which was founded by William Merritt Chase. He joined the faculty in its seventh season and found it a good fit. The two men complemented each other with their counterpointed instruction. Chase felt that delicate detail was the essence of art, while Henri was after motive and a spontaneous recording of everyday life. He sent his students out on the streets of New York City to find their material rather than having them default to stuffy interiors or staid still lifes.

In 1909, he founded the Henri School of Art, which enrolled over a hundred students the first semester. While he became fastidious about his own studio, keeping paints and brushes clean and organized, he always provided his students with a rich classroom environment. The shelves held a repository of leftover paint, and the walls were covered in sepia photographs of paintings by his favorite artists in an ever-changing gallery. Windows were thrown open wide to allow in the noise of the streets below. He often invited members of Isadora Duncan's dance troupe to pose in their elegantly draped Grecian gowns, along with friends from the world of theater. He hoped that by creating a lively setting, he'd help his students feel free to express themselves and find their individuality.

By 1910, Henri was one of the most powerful influences in the New York art world; his paintings were regularly sought after for sales and exhibitions. His classes were filled with the next generation of artists, whose work was exhibited along with his own at the famed Armory Show and whose names appeared in the pages of *Who's Who in American Art*.

As the years went on, his students encouraged him to write down his thoughts on painting. One student even took notes. He turned his instruction sheets, class notes, letters from former students, and critiques of their work into his treatise *The Art Spirit*. With Lippincott as his publisher, he set the price at two dollars so that it was affordable to the average student. The book became required reading in art classes during the 1920s and 1930s. Most memorably, he wrote, "As I see it, there is only one reason for the development of art in America, and that is that people of America learn the means of expressing themselves in their own time and in their own land. In this country we have no need of art as a culture; no need of art for poetry's sake, or any of these things for their own sake. What we need is art that expresses the spirit of the people today."

The art spirit that Henri so richly displayed in his life, work, and teaching is evident in the eleven stories collected in *The Talent: Stories of Authors and Artists*. The world of the arts—visual, literary, and performing—is suggested in all its complexity. The stories dramatize what Henri strongly believed: life in the arts was a vocation above all others, and creative production, despite its sacrifices and challenges, offered moments of joy and discovery.

Visual artists abound in this collection. Martin, the abstract sculptor in Lauren Acampora's "Swarm," has slipped into an unproductive retirement. He admits that he has been "resting on his laurels," when a wealthy new neighbor commissions him to turn his home into an art project. He sees in this opportunity "the improbable pinnacle of his career." The frenzy of covering a house in swarms of rubber insects moves into obsession, with a tragic yet strangely life-affirming outcome. Artists in the making, one a woodworker, the other a painter, also lapse into obsession in Gabrielle Hovendon's "A Quiet Pilgrimage to Every Last Ruined Saint." Zhivka and Sasho meet as teenagers while growing up in a grim housing block in Eastern Europe. The story chronicles their efforts to use art to escape their painful and reductive worlds.

"Door to Everything," by Frank Montesonti, finds Claire, a second-rate artist and granddaughter of a famous painter, making easy money painting the kind of art people hang over their couches. When sales dry up, she must find an even less expensive apartment. She rents one with a door opening onto a mauve void, what the Realtor calls "the door to everything." As she begins to explore what's beyond the door, it invigorates her life and art and offers experiences beyond her imagination that for a time transforms her art. "The Pickers" by Ernest J. Finney features an artist who uses her talent to forge rare manuscripts and artwork. Tracy, the daughter of a single mother who supported them as a junk dealer, inherits her mother's rare talent for haggling and gamesmanship. Despite her success, she is becoming weary of the antiques business. Her crowning achievement is the successful sale of a set of Modigliani drawings, a sale that leads to a stunning personal transformation and a new life of her own making.

Stories of writers fill these pages as well. In M. G. Stephens's "The Prodigal Daughter," Eileen, an Irish poet, gave up her career to follow her husband, a noted Cuban jazz musician, around the world. Now, in late middle-age as a recovered drug addict, she returns to Ireland to help her sisters tend to their dying mother. It becomes clear that Eileen was her mother's favorite. She admired her daughter's choice of adventure over domesticity, a revelation that fills her siblings with wrath and envy and Eileen with a sense of acceptance as she understands that in the end her choices were risky but the right ones. The would-be writer in Becky Mandelbaum's "Babette Has Gone Missing," is tired of servitude to a husband and two sons. As a means of escape, she dashes off a story that wins her an artist residency in the Southwest. The freedom allows her to revel in the pleasure of writing a novel and having an affair with a handsome screenwriter who proves to be more adept at the lighthearted romance of residency hookups than she. Her novel succeeds, but in ways she could never have imagined.

The actors in Catherine Gammon's "Ursula and Will" meet as nearly famous actors on a Netflix series. The story traces the rise and fall of their careers and their on-again-off-again romance as they navigate the complexities of identity and self. It's a story of powerful desire for both love and work and how the two might at times be out of sync. Additional stories in this collection dive deep into the lives and work of an editor, a photographer, and a textile artist. These stories invariably show that the arts, in all their variety, are intertwined with the lives of their makers.

When Robert Henri died in 1929, he left behind more than four thousand paintings. Many were destroyed by his sister-in-law, who became his executor. She believed such a large body of work would dilute the value of his best work, so she burned 550 pieces that she deemed inferior. While friends, students, and critics were horrified when they learned of this, they also knew that Henri had concerned himself very little with the business of art. He said, "I am not interested in art as a means of making a living, but I am interested in art as a means of making a life."

K. S. & S. M.

Ursula and Will

Catherine Gammon

They were minor stars. They met on the set of a series that was shooting in a castle near Prague. They should have been famous. The series was brilliant and maintained a following, especially once it dropped on Netflix. But their timing was bad, or luck, or the choices they made.

Now they lived together and did odd jobs to make ends meet. Sometimes she got a commercial. He accepted an almost invisible role in a single episode of something or other for network TV and died in the opening scene. She barely saw his face, even when they brought him back later as a body on a slab in the morgue. When they weren't acting, they temped, incognito, or waited tables, or cooked with a catering crew, careful that the restaurant or gig wasn't one likely to draw people from the industry. They still collected residuals. They still had agents. But they had effectively disappeared.

They were young enough that they could have made another life, but tenaciously held on, to their hopes and ambitions, to their sense of their own beauty, to their love for one another. When they were desperate, they sat together in bed watching their still only somewhat younger selves fall in and out of and again in love. In the series they had played a brother and sister, driven by sensual passion and abhorrence of incest—vampires, metaphoric, not literal. They had played their scenes against the real desire they felt for one another and resisted throughout the three seasons of intermittent shooting, all the way to the finale, when he did or didn't die but either way irrevocably left her.

She had always let herself believe that his character lived, her only evidence the closing shot of the series and his presence beside her in the bed.

At last, at the end of shooting, they had surrendered to the thirst and mystery of their bodies. On set, they had been naked together on several occasions, enacting scenes of unrealizable fantasy, but now their bodies were their own, no longer images, not for sale, and they were free. Still, the traces of their several years of fictional life hung around them, like a gauze, she thought, a silk. A spider's web, he said. Or your hair. They played their parts in bed together, uneasily, unhappily, until slowly, in their bodies, they found themselves again and their fictional selves began at last to fade.

They did no work during that time, despite the concerns and pleas and warnings of their agents.

"I have a history of stopping short," Will said.

"You're too young to have a history," Ursula said.

"No, really," he said. "In my senior year of high school I signed up to do an independent project in place of taking three core classes, and instead of doing the work I spent all my time with a girlfriend until the last week when I churned out a barely passing paper. When my dad was teaching me to drive, the first corner I turned I blew out a tire and never drove again."

"How can you live in LA and not drive?"

"Uber, Lyft," he said. They hadn't yet returned to the city, not together.

"I rejected the first role they offered me," he said. "I was still a kid. My parents let me say no."

"Lucky for me," she said.

"Maybe not. We'd be sitting pretty. As my dad used to say."

"Like, *When our ship comes in*?"

"That, too."

"Our dads were sort of the same, then."

"Don't go there," he said. He let the implication sink in before he continued. "I pull out of things before they're done."

"Not with me, you don't," she said, as if a sexual joke could disarm his worry. Fail, she thought. "And don't even think *Not yet*. History isn't destiny."

In Los Angeles, living together, sort of, in the apartment she kept with another aspiring and often absent actor, alone together one night as they ate Thai food in bed and watched themselves perform their Renaissance love story with the volume set on mute, she said, mid-episode, "They warned my sister not to marry the man with the bright red car, the steel-toed boots, the little goatee. They told her to give it up, to let him go. But she wouldn't listen. She packed her bags and ran off with him. She's the happiest person I know."

"Like you and me," he said.

She shrugged and turned the sound up as a scene they had shot together began. When it was over they made love, slow and silent, as if her absent housemate was awake in the next room, or as their fictional selves, caught in a nightmare.

"To not make a sound is absurd," he said afterward. "Sound

is what we are. Breath is sound. Blood is sound. Muscle and bone and skin and pain and pleasure. Or maybe the problem is in the making, the not—"

"Hush," she said and put her fingers to his lips.

On a weirdly wet hot afternoon they walked on the beach, sand fleas popping on and off and up and down her naked legs. "I remember a house full of fleas when I was a child," she said. "A tattered couch, faded, rough, teal. I was ashamed of the fleas and the tattered couch. I remember the cats we had then and how they loved us. I remember the sound of my father whistling."

"I think we're done," he said. "I think we need to move on."

"Move on," she repeated. People were walking or sunbathing all around them, but not so many as there would have been if the air had been cooler or dryer or the beach free of fleas.

"The agents are right," he said.

"Really?" she said. "Last night we were getting married."

"That's never going to happen," he said.

When she didn't respond, he walked away and into the waves, cutting through the salty water until she couldn't see his legs, and at last he turned to face her. "Come on," he called, "wash away the fleas," and when she reached him, he pulled her hard against his body and groped her under the water, fingers sliding between the binding of her bathing suit and her skin and finding her, pushing deeper in. He bit her lip and turned her and pressed against her from behind and kissed her neck and ear and probed until he was fucking her, water splashing with and around them, rolling in and rolling out, hiding and revealing, until, satiated, they collapsed to the soaking sand and let themselves be washed over, held their breaths and surrendered to being swept in from the deep and back to land.

She had not believed him when he said it was over, but that act of sudden sex on the beach turned out to be their last, at least for a time. "Someone is asking a question no one can answer," he said as she drove home. "Every groping for an answer is another question, every answer a refusal. When? What? Why? Why not?"

In the morning he packed a bag.

He was going on a shoot, a freebie, supporting some indie director, starring in her short, a showcase for festivals and grant applications. For a moment Ursula was jealous of this woman. "No, no," he said, and she believed him. He was always doing shorts and student films and artists' experiments for which he never got paid. What difference did it make? They were who they were, she thought. They would always be who they were for each other.

He was gone for five days, as expected, and then for another five.

In his absence she found time to see her agent. She allowed her agent to awaken, if only briefly, her interest in taking another series role. She sat for fresh headshots and saw in them a new and beautiful sadness.

When Will came home he packed everything that was his and moved half a mile away, back to the room he kept in another apartment with other mostly absent actors.

Occasionally they still served together at parties—for the aerospace industry or transportation, bioscience, gas and oil, steering clear of music, arts, entertainment, politics. Even so, they were too often almost recognized, despite her simpler makeup and hair, despite his clean-shaven face and the absence of his best-known character's long black curls. It never happened when she worked without him or to him when he worked without her, only when they stood and moved together through one of these busy rooms where they were meant to be invisible as furniture, merely functional in their black-and-white or sometimes red uniforms, offering trays. Instead, in a room together they rearranged space. A pulse, an urgency, palpable, as if in a show of magic, revealed them in all their glamour as their fabulated selves. Inevitably someone saw. Often a loner, an introvert, a man or woman standing off to the side of the loudly or softly chattering crowd, scanning, watching. Ursula could see the change in such a person's attention and would find an escape before the seeing became a certainty. But now and then she failed, missed the person or the sign. One night a banker slipped her his card. He wanted them to perform for him, privately. He wanted to watch. At a wedding reception under spot lit palm trees, a woman stared at her and then at Will and back at her, and hours later, after their cleanup, they found the woman drunk in the road, waiting to follow them home. At a corporate headquarters high above the city lights, a man in Buddy Holly glasses backed her up against a wall and said, "I know who you are." She denied it. "What are you doing working this party?" She continued to deny it, inching away from him without success, obstructed by a big potted banana plant, until all at once Will was there, yanking Buddy Holly by the shoulder, away from her, a fist in his face. The plant crashed along with the man. Broken glass, champagne and flutes, shocked guests, a retreat to the kitchen, a caterer torn between laughter and rage, too high to care. They forfeited their pay for the night and found a new service to temp for.

"We should try to not work together," Ursula said on the street.

"I don't know," Will said. "I thought that was kind of fun."

She drove him home and dropped him off, without an agreement or even a kiss.

Usually when he left her, even now, he gave her something to take away—a word, a sensation, an image to tease herself with, a touch, a hint, an allusion. That night there was nothing.

The next time she saw him, he was married.

She got serious about finding another role and took every word of advice her agent gave. She sat for another round of photos, going for a harder edge to balance the wistfulness of the previous set. She enrolled again in acting classes, designed for professionals only. Will continued accepting small parts in quirky little indie projects, comedies mostly, in which he never presented himself as the man she knew he was. As if he had lived a lifetime's worth of ambition and darkness as her haunted brother and was now as done with that complex, driven character as he was done with her. As if he could escape them both just by taking off his spectacular wig.

They had let him keep the wig. Multiple wigs, actually. Mementos of the show.

Someday, maybe, they would be worth a fortune. But only if he allowed himself to become a star.

And his wife, the woman he'd married, wasn't even in the business. She taught third grade. He'd met her visiting her classroom to do a puppet play for the kids.

He lived across town with her now and Ursula rarely saw him. She threw herself into the search for real work, and after accepting a part in the ensemble cast of a Netflix series developed from an old line of comic books, she spent hours every day with a trainer when she wasn't up in Canada shooting. Her makeup was garish, and no matter how broad and bad she played, she was told to play broader and badder, an instruction she found both liberating and annoying, but the money and exposure were better than she had seen in years, and once the series dropped, when Will came by to congratulate her, he stayed to binge the first season, eating Thai food with her side by side in bed, for old times' sake, he said.

Before he left, he told her he was leaving his wife. He had not been unfaithful to her or she to him. But he was bored. With everything, he said. It wasn't his wife's fault, but he was a weight on her, bringing her down. To marry her had been a mistake. His mistake. As if he could evade his fate. He had gone back to school. He was studying philosophy and history, he said, when he wasn't volunteering on somebody or other's student film.

In his absence, Ursula had been careful to avoid relationships. She had had sex with a few men, hookups from the catering world, strangers from one of those random gigs, one-time encounters half anonymous, never with anyone who knew her or ever could know who she really was, never leaving an electronic trail. She did not permit herself surrender beyond the physical, and now that she had a public face again, her options for one-off sex were even more limited. She no longer shared an apartment but rented a small house on a hillside and filled it with plants and a pair of cats and hired a sitter to live in it whenever she was away. Will haunted her fantasies, where she dwelled in her imaginary of him, lover and brother from a simpler and more beautiful world. His breakup with his wife hadn't brought him any closer, and Ursula was often away in Vancouver shooting the second season, which was longer than the first. As her character's arc gained complexity, she was allowed at last, for a while, to wipe the clownish blood-red lips off her face, but months later, when Will showed up with takeout to binge the drop with her, calling it a new tradition and wearing black silk and denim, his hair long, darker than its natural color and thickened, "Are you in costume?" were the first words out of her mouth.

"You sound like her," he said.

She knew who he meant. "I *am* her. Her voice is my voice."

He started talking at her, in convoluted academic language, about power and menace, parody and kitsch, comparing comic-book characters, comic-book colors and costumes, comic-book plots, with plots and characters drawn from historical records, costumes and colors nuanced and modeled on centuries of art.

She laughed at him with her comic-book character's stiletto laugh. "Are you trying to grow your wig? Do you intend to be my brother forever?"

They almost fought but backed off, settled down into her pillows and muted their phones to watch, uninterrupted, all fourteen hours of her show's second season. After her character's foray into vulnerability, by the finale she was painted red again—her mask, though a little more lifelike, as impenetrably enameled as before. When it ended, they fell asleep together with the cats at their feet, and when they woke up the next afternoon, they almost made love.

The Will waking beside her, faux-black hair tousled, with Thai food on his breath, was a lazy imitation of the dangerous, driven lover of her deep desire and devotion. A caricature. He smiled as if a smile was all he needed to win her back, or over. Where was the suffering? The ambition? Buried under layers of kind gesture and graduate-student mannerism? He had wanted to conquer the world. Or at least their world.

"I never meant to be a star," he said, trying to explain himself. "That was you, Ursula. That was all you."

But she didn't believe him. He had been brilliant in the part of her brother.

"The writers made him," Will said. "The period, the history. The wigs. He wasn't me."

"You weren't unhappy then," she said. "All that time. You weren't drifting the way you are now. Do you still have an agent?"

He shrugged and tried to change the subject, to get her out of bed, to feed the cats, to shower, to dress, to go out somewhere for dinner.

"I don't want to go out. Everyone knows me out there again."

"Don't kid yourself," he said. "Nobody knows you. Not even your name. They only know that ridiculous character."

His cruelty confused her. "And what about you? What do they know about you?"

"Me?" he laughed. "My pretty face?"

She asked why he was dyeing his hair. He was reluctant but finally answered. "Part maybe. Superhero movie. Ensemble."

She waited for more, but "Jinx," he said, shaking his head.

"I don't know you," she said. "I don't know you at all."

"Did you ever?"

When the wind slammed in from the east, the endless over dry heat intensified their longing for adventure, for change, for sex. They drove, mostly. She drove. Into the hills or up the coast or down to the beach. Drove in circles, drove wherever speed allowed her, and day after day he rode beside her. They avoided the city and all its playgrounds. She blew her trainer off. The desert was good. She drove straight into it, the heat and the wind, and the air in the desert was cooler. They thirsted; they didn't know for what. Not for each other. They went to the movies. They went to a club. They ate. They drank. They danced. They played cards. They gambled. They went to the races. *Off to the races*, her father used to say every day on his way to work. "No one talks like that anymore," she said. They were walking in the park. They called it hiking. They saw a mountain lion. In her yard they saw deer, a coyote, a rabbit, a feral cat. The wind died but the air stayed hot, and the sky filled with the smoke and pinks and reds and oranges of wildfires. Birds still liked her trees, out of reach of the cats. A fog rolled in. After Thanksgiving, he didn't go back to school. When the rains came, the cats flew into the house, still wild, still chasing one another and the mouse they'd lost inside the stove. The rains brought flood and mudslides.

They still had not made love.

"Nothing is simple anymore," she said.

"We live in a desert," he said. "A desert canyon surrounded by desert mountains, a desert basin opening on a desert beach. We wait for the hot wind and when the wind comes we wait for the rain and when the rain comes we pray for it to end. Nothing we know can survive the fires and heat and rising ocean, and even though we know this we just go on and on."

They still had not made love, and then they got busy again with work.

By the time he came to watch season three with her, he was married to someone new, already divorcing, and the superhero film in which he had played a small but standout supporting role was in postproduction. She had started season three as something like a superhero herself, then passed through an incarnation as a ghoul. By the end she didn't know what she was—fallen monster, victim, saint. She began to wonder how much longer she could play this character and fantasized advocating for her death in the coming season.

She had other friends and she knew he did too, but their worlds of friends were separate from their life together. A life together, she thought. What a strange idea it was. Their annual comic-book-series binge, their desert drives. She saw his movie without him, more than once. She liked it better at home than on the big screen. She would have seen everything she loved about him in his small performance but for its exceptional sexlessness. Then he asked her to be his date for the Oscars.

"You know what that would mean?" she said.

"We'd be seen together? Photographed together? Talked about?"

"What? You want that?" The idea troubled her, not because she wouldn't enjoy being on display with him again, an opportunity to play their old desire in public, before cameras, to pretend to be pretending. What bothered her was his interest in it, his willingness—she couldn't find his motive. "Why?" she asked, but his only answer was "Why not?"

"We'd have to check with the agents," she said. She had not told anyone she was seeing him, least of all her agent.

"They'll love it," he said. "We'll play it for the romance."

"They won't love it. They'll be afraid of another disappearance into catering gigs and anonymity."

"Let them," he said and made a horror-film face at her and horror-film hands. "Be afraid," he said. "Be very afraid." He laughed. "Wear that campy lipstick. I'll wear one of the wigs. We can dress in matching outfits. White shirts with plunging necklines and ruffles and flounces, voluminous sleeves. Skinny black leather pants, hooded red cloaks, boots to the knees. I'll stick to you like glue."

"I don't want to play that kind of part with you."

"What then?"

"Real," she said. "Like a drive in the desert. A job to pay the rent. We were serious once."

"You don't know me," he said. "We can get a deal out of this if we play it right."

"A deal," she repeated.

"Together," he said. "We can work together again."

"As what? Sardonic vampires?"

"Sexy sardonic vampires. Rock stars. Royalty of rock and roll. There's a vehicle for this waiting out there for us. We'll summon it by showing ourselves, twinned at the hip and thirsting. We can drive in the desert forever if we work together again."

The weirdness of the world sometimes overwhelmed her. He got his rock-star vampire movie. He got her to play the part. They fucked on screen and off. She didn't know who he was, or herself. He had been the unattainable throughout her short working life. When he married for a third time, the ingenue victim of the rock-and-roll vampire queen, Ursula attended the wedding. She celebrated her thirtieth birthday reading a pile of scripts. Better scripts, scripts without garish lipstick or black leather pants. She missed him the most when the hot winds blew and she drove to the desert alone. Her long-running comic-book character was not killed off, but her agent got the producers to write the part smaller and smaller, limiting the time Ursula had to spend in Canada. Will had joined the series—someone's cameo idea run amok. She continued missing the Will of catering gigs and anonymity. She looked for a script that could evoke those days of hiding out in ordinariness and invisibility, a script that would give them a chance to perform it, to manifest that moment when touched by the gods or God their bodies altered space. She wanted that rush when the fire between them blazed and made them visible. She wanted to see it one more time, that instant of transfiguration, captured on film. She wanted to feel it again. In the doing. In the watching. Without the campy trappings. Without the wig or flaming lips. Without the skinny pants or red capes or bustier or black leather boots. Without the fetish-high heels. It would have to be a comedy, she thought. Comedy was the only solution. Just the two of them, alone, ordinary bodies, working a crowd, offering exotic finger foods and flutes of champagne.

Door to Everything

Frank Montesonti

Galleries know there is a certain type of painting that sells, and every gallery has one or two artists whose work isn't exciting or edgy but are kept on because it is nice to know there will be enough income to pay the water bill every month. The average buyer doesn't want five mason jars glued to a steel beam containing all the artist's body hair collected over the span of four years. Most want something to hang over their new Italian couch or in a blank space in the foyer by the stairs. Claire made these paintings. Still lifes mostly, acrylic or oil, heavy brush strokes and bright colors with an expert play of shadow and light. They had enough artistic flourish to give the proper amount of expressionist feeling, but not so much that despair might leak from the canvas into the comfortable rooms of a buyer's brownstone.

This, coupled with the fact that her grandfather was a very famous artist, secured her regular shows where her paintings sold quickly. Her grandfather wasn't just a little famous but a household name whose work demanded millions and hung in the Met. You could find his paintings reproduced in the poster bin in any college bookstore for undergraduates to frame for their dorm-room walls. Little of her grandfather's wealth, however, trickled down to Claire. Her grandfather had had two wives after Claire's grandmother, and her father had sold what paintings he had to fund a series of ill-fated archaeological missions. Because of these missions, Claire had grown up in a random assortment of countries—Morocco, Israel, Bolivia, Sri Lanka—never knowing where home was, exactly, and learning to speak with the slight British accent of the international traveler. So, though she sold everything she made, she barely managed to make enough money to survive on her art in Manhattan, and when her old building went condo, she was forced to find a new place.

She met the Realtor outside a building near Washington Square Park. She liked the Realtor's name, Spieglenik, liked how her gray suit matched her eyes, how she was bent in unlikely ways like a sculpture that had to work around a huge knot in wood or stone. She liked how she seldom spoke and, when she did, how each word felt like calligraphy.

They went upstairs, opened the door, turned on the overhead fluorescent lights. The apartment was a characterless white box. High ceilings and one nice window, but those were the only things remotely special about it. It was small, about five hundred square feet, with one corner blocked off for the bathroom. The only other fixtures were a small stove and a tiny freestanding basin for a sink. It felt more like an art studio than an apartment, exactly what she was looking for.

"This apartment meets your requirements with one exception. There is a door on the back wall that leads to a room that is un-in-hab-it-able."

"What makes it uninhabitable?"

"It would be easier to show you," said Spieglenik.

The Realtor led Claire to a plain white door on the far wall. When she opened the door, there was nothing on the other side except a six-foot-square platform. Around the platform there was empty space that extended, seemingly forever. The empty space was a mauve color.

"What is it?" asked Claire.

"The everything behind everything, around everything. That space."

"But what is it made of?"

"That would be the wrong question to ask."

"Can I go out on the platform?"

"You may."

Claire walked out on the platform. Looking back, she could see the outline of the door, but around it was just more of the mauve space extending in every direction. Then, two eerie feelings in quick succession—the first was the fear that Spieglenik might close the door on her, and the second was the impression that she was standing on nothing and was sure to fall. Her knees buckled, and she stuck out her arms for balance, then got down on all fours.

"I think I'll come in now," she said and crawled back to the door. When she was inside she took a deep breath and tested her weight on the floor.

"It is best if the room is avoided," said Spieglenik.

"I agree," said Claire and shut the door. But other than the odd room, this apartment was acceptable and quite inexpensive for the area, so she signed the lease.

She hauled in all her furniture and supplies. There was so much of it. Boxes of oil paints in different hues. Each tube wrinkled and rolled. Huge tubs of acrylic that she almost never used anymore; a few palettes stuck together. There were her big easels and small. Her lighting so she could freeze shadows in place. There were so many vases and baskets. There were boxes of opalescent stones and glass she collected from the beach. There were taxidermy birds and wax fruit. There were clamps and spools of gleaming wire. There were brushes wrapped in thick blue rubber bands. There were hundreds of sketchbooks; there were primed canvases and half-finished paintings. Then there were the general objects of life. The clear plastic tubs that held her clothes, boxes of books, furniture; and that box full of dead batteries, takeout menus, extension cords, and unopened mail that every move seems to produce.

By the time she was done, there was hardly room to walk through the apartment. Something about the scene depressed her. She remembered a time when moving excited her, when painting excited her, when the very materiality of things excited her: the heft of an expensive tube of oil paint, its shiny metal. The potential of a stack of freshly primed canvases in the corner, the slight ammonia smell of the fresh gesso.

Now, after moving everything, she was intensely aware of weight, of volume, of how many *things* life required. For a moment, she felt them all around her, animated by her, as if she were some gestalt being made of her tools.

Suddenly the new apartment felt stuffy. She opened a window, but it only opened a few inches. It was one of those crank-style windows found in old schoolhouses. Then she remembered her gallery-mate Nicola's show. The gallery was within walking distance now. Everyone liked Nicola's work. The show was expected to be the event of the month. Claire didn't bother getting dressed up. She wore one of her long floral dresses and didn't wash the paint off her knuckles. With the sharp angles of her face and her height, she could have easily done some modeling, but she cared little for her appearance. Men or women seldom approached her because she exuded no sexual signals whatsoever; she was aloof and unapproachable.

When Claire entered the gallery, a waif-thin gallery intern with angelic cheeks poured her a half glass of chardonnay before turning back to her Instagram. Nicola worked in a pop-art style. Claire walked past a piece that was simply a number of emojis lined up like you might see them displayed on a phone, but the emojis were all ways of being killed—an electrocution emoji, an emoji of a slit wrist, a bloody bathtub, and so on. Next to it was a painting of various phallic-looking vegetable emojis and sex acts. The title of the show was "Desperately Needed Emojis." It was clearly a hit. His paintings would hang in the lobbies of tech startups around the city.

Claire knew Nicola as a gallery-mate and considered him a friend. Sometimes they would have a coffee in Central Park, and Nicola would tell her all the gossip about other artists, but now that she thought of it, it had been a year since they had even done that. Tonight, he was the star. He was drinking an enormous smoothie, surrounded by some other artists and a couple of art critics she recognized. It wasn't like her, but she felt a moment of hesitation, like she didn't belong there, couldn't approach her own gallery mate. But when she approached, everything seemed fine. Nicola hugged her. They exchanged exaggerated cheek kisses. Some small talk slipped straight from their mouths into oblivion. Then, as Claire walked away from the group, she heard Nicola say to one of the critics, "Yes, his granddaughter," and she felt a static charge pass through her chest, a tingle in the back of her skull.

The room now had too much input, too much information. She instinctively searched for an escape and slipped into the back office, where she found Susan McCaskill, the gallery owner, one of her grandfather's former students. They might have been lovers. Everyone was lovers back then. Susan was older now, wore her gray hair wrapped in a fantastic twist on the top of her head and her glasses hung from a silver chain around her neck. They hugged and sat down. Claire felt better in Susan's presence, her motherly calm.

"How are the pieces coming?"

Claire just shrugged and gave a half smile.

Susan tucked some hair behind Claire's ear. "Be sure to do some more smaller pieces this time. We need to hit all the price points. I know it's tedious, but that's the business. And please talk to Nicola about getting a web presence, dear," she said as a man with the front half of his head shaved like a Qing Dynasty monk entered the office.

"Paolo, you're back!" Susan erupted and hugged the man.

Claire took that opportunity to slip out. She slid gracefully through the gallery again and entered the warm New York summer night. Once she was outside, the slight anxiety was gone. But relief didn't take its place. It was like nothing ever pressed too hard on her, nothing ever settled, nothing was permanent. When she was a child, she had always been moving, blown place to place. It was as though she had never learned to want. What should she want, after all? The critics to care about her work? To be invited to Nicola's parties? She knew he didn't invite her. Did she want to date, to be *desired*? It felt odd thinking about wanting to be desired. Sometimes it felt like she was made of a material to which nothing could stick. She was never too happy or too unhappy. She was like the vases of flowers she painted, colored as they were born to be colored. If they were lit in a beautiful way, it was by a sun millions of miles distant.

And when she did feel something, why did it have to be this churning feeling of everything mixed together, a tumbled gray rumble? She walked the quiet streets of the Village. So many wealthy people lived here now that the brownstones were often empty while their owners traveled or enjoyed their other homes. She rode the exceptionally tiny elevator up to her apartment. She opened her door. The ambient nighttime city light flowed in the window onto her painting supplies, her stacks of boxes, which rested obediently in the dark where she had left them. She turned on the buzzing overhead fluorescents. She looked at a half-completed painting she had set on an easel. Sometimes she felt the half-completed work was more beautiful than the finished pieces. She liked how the pencil sketch of the flowers seemed to grow from the fully painted avocado; she liked the idea of the armature exposed.

She picked up an avocado from the bowl, admiring its dark-green, puckered skin. She looked at the plain white door on the wall. She walked toward it slowly, as if she felt it necessary to sneak up on it. This time, however, she wasn't scared. She opened the door. It was bright in the room to nothing, or the room to everything, whatever it was. Just the mauve color everywhere, no shadows, no wind or sound. She sat down on the platform cross-legged and looked over the edge. It didn't feel like she would fall. She threw the avocado into the void. It floated away from her, weightless, like it might in space.

She watched it grow smaller until it eventually disappeared. "Hello," she yelled into the void, but there was no echo.

She went back inside and hefted a modestly sized painting that had been finished for several months. This one was some flowers with a fall theme—bare branches, a basket of mushrooms. She took the painting out on the platform. She held it up toward her, as if she were going to hang it on a wall, then gave it the smallest shove out into the empty space so it traveled away from her very slowly, into the void. She might have made three thousand dollars on that painting, but in that moment, it felt like a small price to pay to hang a piece of her work forever in the gallery of oblivion. As she watched it slowly fade away, she started crying. She felt like a mistake in the world, not a person but a gap, a strange interlude or silence, like those moments when you are at a party and for some reason everyone stops speaking at the same instant.

And then something was just *decided* in her.

There is no other way to put it. She was just different, like it had been ordained by something so huge it would be laughable to question. She knew what she had to do. She went back into her apartment and started with the paintings. One by one, she threw them into the void. Then the art books, then her clothes, even the furniture she managed to drag and shove over the edge, so that in the morning she woke up on her twin mattress with nothing left but a few items in the bathroom—razors to remove her body hair, a bright red lipstick, powder for her face. She was tingling all over. She couldn't stop smiling. The air around her was electric but also silent. She had a little vision then. She imagined two strokes of paint on a canvas, felt herself in the silence, the space between the strokes. Then she imagined them farther apart, so far apart the silence became unknowable.

She knew the next step. She stopped resisting and moved as she was pulled. She walked shoeless into a high-end store, spent all her savings on five designer summer dresses, all white, white leggings, white shoes. In her pure white clothing, she felt lighter, like she was only half in this world. She tied her hair back with a simple piece of white kite string. Her desires were entirely with her now that she had shed most of herself.

She walked through the Village until she realized a shape in her mind, a gap, a specific emptiness. She ordered ten large pieces of ebony and borrowed some woodworking tools from her grandfather's sculptor friend, now retired. She spent two weeks creating the first sculpture, which looked like a boat emerging from a rock on black water. Then she made another, a huge comma erupting from the seed of a plant.

When she went out in her new white clothes, she seldom spoke. She would smile at the owner of the café downstairs where she ate almost all her meals. Soon she stopped speaking altogether. She drifted around Central Park and stared at the blue sky, closed her eyes and felt the city sounds push and pull her thoughts. She would walk into corporate buildings where she didn't belong, wide-eyed, touching the leaves of some plant in the lobby or just looking up at the tall glass walls, enraptured, like she had just arrived on this planet from a realm where there was only one type of beauty.

She allowed herself to take lovers, and she took many. She was beautiful, really. Thin, tall, with dark brown eyes and hair. If she found someone attractive, man or woman, she would just look directly at the person and smile—at the park, at a coffee shop, just on the street. They would look away like it was some mistake, but then she would just keep looking, keep smiling, expressing the feeling that she admired them and wanted to know them without cover or deception, just as open truth.

When she brought them home, she would make them disrobe at the door and put their clothes in a white bag hung on a hook by the door. She never called them. She had no phone. If they came back and knocked, she would let them in. If not, she just felt them sweep through her life like a wind. There were so many people in this city, and she was just one; she felt herself sending out her signal to the empty cosmos.

When they hauled in her work for the first show, Susan was furious. Why hadn't Claire told her she was doing something new? All the marketing had been for the other show, and there was no guarantee this would sell, and couldn't she at least get a phone? But Claire just stood in the gallery and looked at her with an expression lacking guilt, shame, or ambition. It was a look that seemed to suggest that all struggle was mainly pointless. And no one knows the vagaries of the world better than an art gallery owner, so Susan just sighed, and they installed the pieces.

Then there was buzz and rumor. Art-world royalty Claire had flipped her lid and screwed the gallery with wild sculpture. It was kind of good, I heard. She was at the Baxter show and wearing all white, acting like a monk, and maybe she was zonked on something, we all thought, but she took home Gerard, you know beautiful Gerard, and he said she made him strip at the door and put his clothes in a white sack on a hook, and she never spoke a word the whole time. He said it was beautiful, really, not speaking, not assuming anything but the moment. He swears she wasn't on anything, just had become a *being of light*.

So, the gallery was packed, and the art critics asked Claire questions, and she just looked at them and didn't respond until they answered their own questions. *Of course, it's what I thought, or maybe not, but it's different, and I understand now*. She moved about the gallery detached but exuding a transcendence that was radiant, and somehow the whole place felt blessed, like everyone there was in a room that wouldn't change, that would float through history and space like an unbreakable unit. Everyone felt it, in the way people do, in the way people feel much more than they can ever say or know. It was a night like that.

Everything sold. Susan was nearly in tears and a little drunk. There would be pictures and a full write-up in the *Times* and *Art Forum*. Claire's old work would surge in value, and then there would be articles about where the promising young artist had disappeared to, rumors of Rome or São Paolo. But she didn't go to those places. After the show, Claire went home and opened the door to everything on her back wall. It was time. Nothing told her it was time; it was just time. There wasn't really any choice. That was like saying the rain has a choice. The sun has a choice. She was blooming toward the final removal.

Only two things were left, the platform and the door. And what an artist she was. Without any fear that she would never come back, she jumped off the platform. Up, up, she went, into the mauve forever, a single mark of contrast on a canvas with no edges, the very first stroke of creation.

Swarm

Lauren Acampora

The new house was a horror. Martin and his wife remarked on it each time they turned onto Minuteman Road and were struck by the bald ostentation. The house, constructed in just three months, appeared to have been modeled after a Palladian villa. It was fronted by a columned entry with a pediment like a dunce cap, and its symmetrical wings were shot through with fussy, arched windows. Although the structure was set back from the road, the owners had perversely removed the trees at the property's front edge and installed a squat stone wall flecked with mica. Neither of them was typically prone to prejudgment, but Martin and Philomena considered themselves people of modest leanings and allowed themselves the small, wicked gratification of condemning the owners' taste.

And so Martin detected a tone of abashment in his wife's voice when, over dinner, she told him she had met their new neighbors.

"The wife's name is Sheryline," she said between bites. "I was driving past and she was out by the mailbox, so I stopped to say hello. Anyway," Philomena sighed, "she seemed very nice. Maybe in her midfifties."

"Fifties?"

"They just moved up from the city. Their kids are already grown."

"You mean it's just the two of them?" Martin said. "In that palazzo?"

"Yes, I guess so." Philomena sighed again. "Anyway, I invited them over for Saturday. It seemed the natural thing to do."

"I wish you would've asked me first."

"Why? What would you have said? No?"

Martin looked down to the burnt-orange cross-hatching of the chair upholstery, then back up to his wife. She was in her usual spot, across from him at the table, her plump form silhouetted by the window behind her, gilded with late-afternoon sun. Her hair shone white gold.

Martin had seen forty years of skies pass by that window. The interior of the dining room was still lined with wood paneling, as it had been the day they had moved in. Like a ski lodge. He had stared at the same wooden slabs for forty years, too, his eye settling on their natural flaws, the dark knots in the grain like stationary whirlpools. Forty winters in this room, with chili and cocoa. The zero sound of snow. The shifting, lenticular sky.

In the summer, Philomena's garden opened like a garden in a children's book. Her climbing-rose trellis bloomed, then the diagonal rows of marigold. The little pond in the woods came alive with turtles and frogs. And over those forty years, property values had blossomed, too. Their three-bedroom colonial with green shutters and charmingly darkened shingles was now worth at least a million dollars. Nearly a full acre on a desirable street between train line and school. If this was possible—if it was possible that a boy who'd sucked licorice on the sidewalks of Flatbush could be a millionaire now, inflation notwithstanding—then the world was a spooky and fabulous place indeed.

Martin had hated the house at first. It took him too far from the city and the cramped studio on 14th Street that he'd come to romanticize. He enjoyed watching the restless parade of crooks, bums and nuns beneath his window. He enjoyed putting a canvas against a wall and making brutish marks that clanged like music. But this house had endeared itself to him over the years. The rooms had absorbed something of him, and he of them. And he knew that it had been a fortunate confluence of timing and geography that had softly deposited him upon a tenure track at the state university, just a twelve-minute drive from Minuteman Road.

They'd grown fairly close to some of the neighbors, a handful of couples with children the same age as theirs with whom they took turns hosting dinners. Martin always had the feeling that these gatherings were building toward some ultimate consummation of friendship that hovered just one or two dinners away. The Loomises had been the first to sell. They traded their lovely, weatherworn home on the Sound for a Spanish-tiled monster in Jupiter. The Petries were next, once their children were safely launched onto Wall Street. For them it was Sanibel Island. Then the Henrys and Callahans. They all fell, as if to gravity, to that southerly force so much like the grip of death. They all bequeathed their houses to sweet, anxious families like mirror images of their younger selves.

Philomena had broached Florida just once, and just once Martin had said *never*.

After dinner, he helped his wife with the dishes, then retired to the studio. In one corner, a sawhorse sat idle. In another, a tower of brittle sketchbooks leaned into the wall. The easel wore a thin pelt of dust. Martin settled into the worn easy chair and opened an issue of *Time* magazine. A fly orbited his head, alit on his ear, clung. There was the brief, eerie feeling of miniature appendages taking purchase on flesh before his hand rose reflexively. The fly found a perch on the edge of the gummed-up turpentine jar, and Martin sank deeper into his chair. He skimmed the pages of *Time* and napped, as had become his evening ritual.

The Gregorys came on Saturday. Sheryline was a doll, he had to admit, with a fit body beneath her pink sweater and pedal pushers. He shook her hand firmly—he was still a robust man and wanted to demonstrate this—and returned her smile with a handsome set of teeth, still his own. The husband, too, Martin found likable. John Gregory wore a pair of plaid golf pants with a brass-buttoned blazer. His collar parted to reveal the pink flesh of a happy businessman. It seemed impossible that these were the philistines behind the nouveau concoction on the corner.

They exchanged pleasantries and took seats around the wooden coffee table that still bore the scars of children's homework. Philomena served tall glasses of Campari and soda with lemon crescents. Sheryline and John shared the old brown couch, and their hosts flanked them in armchairs.

"So," John leaned forward toward Martin, "Philomena tells us you're an artist."

"Oh." Martin glanced at his wife. "Well, yes."

"What kind of work do you do?" Sheryline chimed.

Martin looked again toward Philomena, who returned his glance with an encouraging smile.

"Well, I've always been a painter, primarily," he began, "but really I've dipped into everything."

"The Carnegie Museum owns one of his paintings." Philomena swirled her glass. "So does the Menil Collection in Texas."

"Really?" Sheryline put down her Campari. "I wonder if we may have seen your work."

"Oh, probably not. It hasn't been on view in a while," said Martin, sipping his drink too quickly, the rhubarb syrup delightfully bitter.

"Do you work here at home?" asked John.

Martin nodded.

"Could we—" John looked at Philomena, "come visit the studio sometime, maybe have a tour?"

Martin clung to his drink and considered for a moment its wedge of lemon, curled at the rim like a banana slug. He put the glass down and stood.

"Well, why not. Let's go do it now."

For a moment he stood alone, fearing that he'd misread the moment. This was the time for dinner, of course, not a studio visit. But the Gregorys stood, and then his wife. He led them through the breezeway to the studio, which had once been the garage.

He began with the vertical painting rack. One by one he slid the few dusty old abstracts into the light and perched them on the easel. The Gregorys made complimentary noises. Then he moved to the later, experimental sculptures, arachnid shapes. There were many more of these to show, their production having aligned with the art world's lamentable shift toward performance and politics. He'd been offered only two solo shows between 1970 and 1985. After that, his gallery had relegated him to summer group exhibitions, then ceased to invite him at all. He tried not to mind this. He had no reason to complain, having earned a comfortable living from teaching, having raised two children to adulthood, having stayed happily married. He had retained his health well into retirement, and although he'd never warmed to golfing, he had found ways to stay occupied. It made no sense to generate more art at this point. It would only take up space.

"Martin, this is phenomenal work," John said gravely.

"We're art collectors, you know," Sheryline added. "So, this is very exciting for us."

"What are you working on now, if I may ask?" John's eyes scanned the room.

"Well, to be honest, I've been resting on my laurels." Martin chuckled. "Just a few drawings here and there." He cleared his throat, paused. "I've always wanted to try something large-scale but it's a question of space. And funding."

John and Sheryline were quiet. Philomena stared.

"Let me ask you something," said John, turning to face Martin, his hands thrust into plaid pockets. "If you had a commission, let's say, and could do any project you wanted right now, what would you do?"

There was a long pause. In a dresser drawer upstairs, beneath his underpants, Martin kept the carefully drawn plans from his youth. The papers were yellowed and the pencil lines faded, but the finished image remained bright in his mind. When he'd proposed the idea to his dealer years ago, he'd received a look of amused incredulity—an unfair response, given the blatant hoaxes other artists were permitted to get away with. It was true that the idea might have seemed a departure, but to Martin it was a natural extension of his vision, its shadow side. He rarely thought of the project anymore, but every so often it appeared to him in a dream, magically realized, and he felt an exhilaration so complete it brought tears to his eyes.

He stood for another moment, looking at John and Sheryline Gregory. Then he went out the studio door and hurried upstairs to his underwear drawer.

The Gregorys returned the next week to formally commission the work. After their visit, Philomena had been strangely quiet. In front of the bathroom mirror, she put her toothbrush down and finally spoke. "Are you crazy? Do you understand how big their house is?"

Yes, Martin said, he was aware of the size. It was perfect. Monumental. He'd seen the excitement in John Gregory's eyes when he unfolded the first drawing. Yes, Martin had explained, those *were* insects, each individually sculpted and affixed to the exterior of a house. Spiders, moths, beetles, grasshoppers. The house in the picture was a generic 1950s ranch, nearly obscured by a mass of clinging bodies, an enchanting tangle of wings, legs and antennae.

"You'd need millions of them to cover it," Philomena said. "Who's going to model each one?" Martin brushed his teeth calmly.

"And the Gregorys are lunatics, too. Who do they think they are? The de Médicis?"

"What's wrong with that?"

Philomena looked at him in the mirror. They locked eyes for a moment, and her face softened. "I just don't want to see you disappointed."

"That won't happen."

"I hope you're right."

"They're serious about this. You heard what they said. They'll cover the cost of materials and pay me the rest when it's finished." Martin smiled at himself. "This could be really big. Hell, it can't be anything *but* big."

"I'm just saying you should measure the house first. You're not twenty-five anymore. You've never even done an outdoor project before."

Martin seized his wife's soft body. He kissed her forehead and bent her backward, hearing the faint click of her bones. "You worry too much," he said.

John Gregory gave him a copy of the blueprints, but Martin barely looked at them. He understood that the house was large; he didn't need to know the exact square footage. First he would need a stockpile of closed-cell foam, dense enough to carve and score. At the lumberyard, he put in an order for a hundred sheets of pink insulation board. From the hardware store, he bought spools of black electrical wire and tubes of foam adhesive. The owner called a supplier in California for a roll of fine-gauge stainless mesh. Lastly, he bought paint. Gallons of all-weather coating in a spectrum of colors. He already had a stack of nature books, including a five-pound insect encyclopedia with color illustrations of specimens cataloged by continent.

After the insulation sheets arrived and the men deposited them in the backyard, Martin sat at the kitchen table with a glass of lemonade. Outside, a mountain of pink foam waited beyond the marigolds, topped with cinder-block weights. He felt giddy, feverish to begin.

"I hope you're not planning on leaving that there," said Philomena, coming through the kitchen in gardening gloves. "It'll kill the grass."

"Don't worry, they won't be there for long."

On Friday, Martin began to make the first bug. He went outdoors, sawed a chunk from a sheet of foam and clamped it into the vise on his workbench. With coping saw, he shaped the piece, then refined it with an X-Acto knife and sandpaper. Then he carved textured ribbing along the thorax and abdomen. After lunch, he cut wing shapes from the stainless mesh and carefully glued wire to their undersides, creating the illusion of veins. Finally, he pierced the thorax with six thick wires: three sets of legs. When Philomena called him for dinner, he had not yet begun painting.

He finished the first insect at ten o'clock that night. There'd been a few setbacks after dinner—a lost leg, a vein peeled away from its wing—but nothing Martin hadn't been able to rectify with invisible glue. Finally, he set about painting the iridescent dragonfly body. Although he was yawning by the time he finished, adrenaline coursed through his bloodstream. He fairly jogged up the stairs holding the piece and carried it to Philomena in bed.

"What do you think?" he panted, holding the insect in front of her. "It's a blue darner, *Aeshna cyanea*."

She looked up from her book. "It's wonderful."

"That's all?"

"It's lovely. But at this rate, it's going to take you ten years to finish."

Martin was silent, holding the dragonfly. "It'll go faster once I get in the swing of things."

Philomena smiled and went back to her book.

"Or if I had an assistant," Martin put a hand to his wife's shoulder.

"You can put an ad in the paper," she said without looking up.

By Tuesday, Martin had completed two dragonflies, two spiders, and one perfect ladybug. On Wednesday, Philomena agreed to help glue the wings to a gypsy moth, and by the weekend she was sitting with him through whole days, helping to carve new creatures from scratch. The production doubled, then tripled—as Martin had predicted it would—as they became more adept. Together, they fell into a kind of shared trance, bending wires and sculpting foam as the summer progressed and weeds crawled up the sides of the pink pyramid behind the house.

Slowly, they produced each species in the book. Despite her bad back and creeping arthritis, Philomena worked unflagging hours, fashioning the spiky hairs on fly legs, painting the chartreuse wings of a luna moth. She worked with a beatific look on her face, like a woman deep in her knitting. By September, they had made a hundred insects. Martin was reluctant to store them in boxes, where they might be damaged. Instead, they rested upon every available surface, until they crowded the studio and overflowed into the breezeway. *Swarm*, Martin decided, would be the title of the piece.

When the Gregorys invited them for dinner, Martin and Philomena walked down Minuteman Road to the glittering stone wall. On foot, the house was more imposing than ever—6,000 square feet at least. Martin said nothing as his wife glanced at him and pressed the musical doorbell.

John led the tour of the interior, pausing to highlight the artwork. The paintings tended to be oversized, lacking in nuance. The artists' names were unfamiliar. Several gallery pedestals surrounded the dinner table, supporting bronze blobs. Martin sat quietly beneath the vaulted ceiling as the others conversed and a chef served steak tartare.

Martin chose not to return the dinner invitation, despite Philomena's protests. It was unwise to give his patrons a preview of the piece before it was complete, he argued, and it would be too much trouble to stow it away.

By November, a phalanx of insects occupied the kitchen. The first snow came and laid a clean blanket upon the hill of insulation boards. Alone in the house, Martin and Philomena slid into the timeless ski-lodge feeling. With the exception of supermarket cashiers and hardware-store clerks, they spoke only to each other. From time to time, there were phone calls, the ring resounding like a siren through the house, making Martin leap. Philomena spoke to their daughter, Melinda, divorced in San Francisco, and their son, Claude, living in Nashville with their two granddaughters.

"Will we come down there for Christmas? he wants to know."

Martin did not respond. He had resorted to fingernail scissors for fashioning the knobs of a millipede's body, and his fingers were blistered from it.

"Martin, I just spoke to you."

"I heard you, love. I just don't know the answer yet."

"The answer to whether you'll fly to see your son and grandchildren for Christmas?"

"That's right. I don't know the answer. I don't think they'll be too happy with my bug-making at the dinner table." He chuckled. "I might get foam dust in the turkey."

"What's so funny? Do you think you're funny?"

"Come on, Phil, I'm only joking. I wouldn't really bring my bugs to Nashville." He paused, breathed in. "But I don't think I should go. I've got too much work to do."

His wife stared at him, her eyes searing blue. He looked at his millipede.

"You can go if you want, of course," he added. "I wouldn't want to stop you from going."

"Well, you don't have to worry about that," she said, and heaved herself up from the couch, her gaze fixed on a point in the distance.

After that, Martin worked alone. He became bogged down with a monarch butterfly whose colors were coming out muddy. It was important, he knew, to create a few really vibrant pieces. Among the monochromes of the insect world, there was always an occasional peacock—a spirit-lifting splash of color. He repainted the butterfly's wings, then put them aside to dry before setting to the delicate task of adding the black veins and spots. As he held the fine-tipped brush, Martin's fingers trembled. He commanded them to steady, but they shook until he was forced to put the brush down.

After breakfast each morning, he went into the studio and sat alone. All around him, arthropods stared with vacant eyes. Their bodies appeared flimsy and childish to him now, the work of a deluded fool. To begin work on a new creature would be to waste another scrap of his life. Whether he'd be better off wasting the same time in Nashville, cramped in his son's frilly guest room, he didn't know. He picked up that week's *Time* magazine and stared at the cover: a soldier poised on a hill in Afghanistan. The world was a mess. This young man, younger than Claude, was baking in the sun, in the sights of hidden rifle scopes. Martin, with his ladybugs, might have been on another planet.

When Philomena startled him awake, he saw that the sun had gone down. He came groggily to the dinner table and looked at his wife. Perhaps she saw the entreaty in his look because the next day she came wordlessly to the studio and helped him again.

They did not go to Nashville. Martin hadn't needed to argue the issue. He'd heard Philomena on the phone one evening. "You know your father," she'd said quietly. "That's true, but still, it means a lot to him." And finally, wearily, "Next year, I promise. But you'll still come up for Easter, I hope?"

They decorated the tree to the songs of Bing Crosby, as was their tradition. Philomena, in an act of goodwill that warmed Martin's heart, eschewed the usual angel and tied his monarch butterfly to the top.

The day before Christmas, the Gregorys surprised them at the front door with a ginger cake.

"Will you come in for tea? A cocktail?" Philomena asked, while Martin scrambled to hide insects in the broom closet.

"No, no, we're on our way to the city," John said. "We just wanted to spread some cheer." He shaded his eyes and peered into the house. "The project going well?"

Yes, of course, Martin assured him. He would be done by New Year's. Philomena glanced at him.

"Wonderful," John boomed. "Well, don't be strangers," he called as they went back out into the snow and climbed into their carriage, a Mercedes SUV.

By the time they finished the last insect, in April, the house was overrun. Together, Martin and Philomena hacked the last lonely pink slab apart where it lay. A flattened yellow patch of grass remained while the rest turned green and Philomena's marigolds sprouted their first leaves.

Martin went on foot down Minuteman Road to report the good news. Although he'd been forced to avoid the Gregorys all winter, his embarrassment evaporated as he inhaled the spring air. He felt almost young as he trotted up their driveway and rang the musical doorbell. And yet he found himself out of breath when Sheryline answered. He gasped, "It's finished."

She wore a look of alarm. "What's finished?"

He laughed, bending to catch his breath. "The project is ready to go. When can we start installation?"

"Come in," she said, smiling, and called for her husband.

They were set to begin work the week before Easter. The timing was bad, Martin admitted. He wanted to see the kids as much as his wife did, but the project couldn't be delayed any longer. He didn't want to lose credibility. Philomena, of course, understood. She calmly went to the phone and asked Claude and Melinda if they could postpone their visits until summer. It would be better this way, Martin assured her. When the project was finished, they'd have time to relax together, to grill outside and go to the beach as a family.

Together, they packed insects into cardboard boxes and loaded the car. The Gregorys had considerately vacated their home for a fortnight's vacation, allowing the artist to work undisturbed. The house was already decked in scaffolding. Anyone passing would have assumed that the new neighbors were simply adding some finishing touches, a few last details to bring the preposterous house completely over the top. Martin smiled to himself. No one would guess the nature of those details. No one would imagine, in a thousand years, the kind of creative risk the Gregorys were about to embrace—the rare kind of people they really were.

It made sense to start at the front, where the impact would be instantly felt, and so they would be sure not to run out of bugs for the façade. Martin gingerly climbed the scaffolding to the top plank of plywood. The platform felt solid enough, but when he glanced at Philomena on the ground, he felt the beginnings of vertigo and clutched a pole.

"Why don't I stay up here, honey, and you can bring the insects up to me a few at a time," he called, keeping his gaze firmly on the bricks of the house. "Just whatever you can handle at once."

Several moments later, he heard the heavy creaking of the scaffolding ladder, and then his wife's hand was there, offering a tarantula. He laughed. "Good place to start."

Philomena continued up and down the ladder each day of the week, and Martin used industrial epoxy to affix the insects to the house at the painstaking rate she brought them up. It was a lot of climbing, he knew, but she did not complain. On Good Friday, she wheezed up the ladder, smiled at Martin, then dipped into her bucket and presented a swallowtail. It was a splendid specimen, zig-zagged with yellow. He found a spot for it next to a cluster of houseflies, where it would glow brilliantly. Philomena balanced patiently at the top rung, gripping the plywood plank with one hand and using the other to unload another insect. Martin reached down for a praying mantis at the moment her grip relaxed. He watched as her fingers released the plank slowly, gracefully, without understanding the meaning of it. Then there was a jangle of scaffolding poles as her body crumpled and dropped to the ground.

Martin felt suspended high above the earth for an instant, saying, "Phil?" even as he moved to scramble down the ladder. The ground was soft, still muddy from spring rain. Philomena lay on her back. Her face was pale, and she looked flatly at him. He began to feel for her pulse, but considered the passing moments and instead ran down Minuteman Road to their home telephone.

When the ambulance came, he rode in the back and watched the medical men. Their huddle obscured his wife from view. He felt absent from the vehicle, as if he was still on the scaffolding platform, holding the praying mantis. He continued to feel absent at the hospital as the doctor laid a hand on his shoulder. *Sudden coronary arrest.* A main artery jammed with plaque, narrowed over the years. Martin walked away from the hospital, through the parking lot and driveway to the edge of the street. Then he turned and looked at the building that held his wife, built of plain white cement blocks. It looked back at him, brutally mute.

The kids stayed with him after the services. Claude and his wife settled into the guest room with their two girls in sleeping bags. Melinda slept on the old brown couch. She dusted the house and vacuumed, sucking up pieces of foam that had found their way into the weave of the rugs. She cooked vegetarian dinners in the wok she'd given them one Christmas, which they'd never used. Martin walked from room to room and sat in every chair. He could not find a comfortable spot. Every place had Philomena in it.

The Gregorys left a condolence card in the mailbox. Martin was glad they hadn't knocked. He remained in pajamas, unshowered. He slept long, dreamless nights and took ugly afternoon naps. He spoke only when necessary. The grandkids grew tired of playing board games and began to whine softly but were chastised by their parents. One morning, Martin walked through the house—past Melinda brewing coffee in the kitchen, Claude and the girls playing outside the window—and went into the studio. There was still a square of insulation board remaining. With the blind motions of habit, he found a serrated knife and carved the tapered abdomen of a wasp.

An unknown period of time passed before his daughter appeared in the doorway.

"What are you doing, Dad?"

"Just keeping my hands busy."

He knew how he must look, the few tufts of dirty white hair fanning out from his head, his pajama top buttoned haphazardly. "Would you like to help?" he asked.

"What do you mean? Help with what?" Melinda stood stoically in a clean black sweater and jeans. There was a tone in her voice that Martin didn't like.

"What do you think? With the project," he answered, keeping his eyes on the bug in his lap.

There was a long pause, and then Melinda spoke with unconcealed rancor. "You have to be kidding me. You're still doing this? Don't you understand that Mom is gone?" His daughter took a breath. "She died, Dad. Doing your stupid project."

Martin did not speak. Melinda turned and left the doorway. He took an X-Acto knife and began scoring the foam.

They were quiet at the dinner table. Melinda forked the salad into bowls with obvious anger, and Claude would not look at his father. At the end of the meal, Martin pushed his chair out from the table and said, "I know what you're all thinking. That I'm a selfish bastard for trying to finish this damn project." His voice quavered, and he glanced at the grandchildren, whose eyes stared back roundly. "But I have a commission, and I'm expected to deliver it. I am a professional."

He took his empty plate to the kitchen and rinsed it, then strode into the studio. A terrible draining sensation took hold of his stomach as he stood in the room, surrounded by insects. Slowly, he filled a cardboard box with painted bodies.

The following day, he drove a loaded car to the Gregorys' house. The draining sensation in his gut had been replaced by something heavy and solid, like an iron brick. He drove up to the scene of his wife's collapse and felt a dull distance, as if he were viewing it through a periscope. He saw, through the periscope's tunnel, that the scaffolding had been removed. A small group of insects clung to the upper corner of the house's face like a mole.

Martin went to the door, clothed in his denim work shirt, and shook John Gregory's hand. He accepted repeat condolences and asked when he might resume work.

The Gregorys cautiously expressed their appreciation that he intended to finish. They consulted briefly, out of earshot. Finally, they agreed to let work recommence, with the condition that they hire workers to install the rest of the piece. Martin, of course, would serve as artistic supervisor.

It felt good to get out of the house. Martin's family had made no move to decamp, nor had they sought rapprochement. The accusation in the air was oppressive. He went out into a fine spring day and walked along the side of the road to the site. The iron brick remained lodged in his gut, and the periscope vision persisted. Far away, he heard a sound that he identified as the lilting calls of birds. The scaffolding was in the process of being replaced by men who did not appear to be artist assistants but a crew of construction workers.

The Gregorys gave Martin a pair of binoculars, with which he could survey the work from a director's chair on the ground, and for several weeks he enjoyed shouting out the names of the insects to the men. Despite their casual manner, the men were prodigious and accurate workers, and Martin watched as, day by day, the house grew a beard of exoskeletons and wings.

At last, in May, Martin's family took their leave. He observed their preparations through the periscope and felt little emotion as they loaded Claude's car with luggage and some of Philomena's things. He knew that he should be affected. He should plead with them to stay, ask for more time to grieve, more consolation. Or perhaps he should ask to accompany them, sell the old house, and live the rest of his days warm and watched over in Nashville. Instead, he bent down to let his granddaughters hug him and waved from the front door as the car backed out of the driveway.

The men affixed the final insect on the last day of May. When they took the tarps and scaffolding down and packed up their equipment, the house looked dazzling in the noon sun. Martin backed away, all the way to the road. Not a glimpse of the original brick was visible. The entire façade was completely and miraculously shrouded in dark, voluptuous texture. Here and there, dashes of color—fuchsia butterfly, lime green caterpillar—popped like jewels. It was exactly, incredibly, the way Martin had imagined it. The manifestation of the house from his dreams, the improbable pinnacle of his career. As he stood at the edge of the driveway, he sobbed like a child.

The Gregorys came out to join him. John patted him on the back and Sheryline held his hand kindly. They were very pleased with how it had turned out, John said. It was a masterpiece; unlike anything they'd ever encountered.

Martin was unable to speak for a moment. "I just wish Phil were here to see it," he said.

Within days, the first phone calls came in. The Gregorys fielded these with aplomb, listening to the neighbors' grievances and politely asserting their own rights as Old Cranbury property owners. They'd been prepared for this kind of reaction, they told Martin. They knew that not everyone shared their avant-garde tastes. With a little time, they predicted, the calls would taper off. People would grow accustomed to the sight, perhaps begin to appreciate its aesthetic value. Eventually *Swarm* might even become a beloved town landmark.

But the calls overflowed to the town hall. The house was a travesty, disgusting to look at. It was bringing property values down. One passerby telephoned in a panic, thinking the creatures were real. The house had already been bad enough, some snapped, but this was a middle finger to the rest of the town. There needed to be regulations to suppress people like the Gregorys who believed the world was theirs to deface.

Finally, Martin read in the *Old Cranbury Gazette* about the lawsuit against his patrons. The art installation was incorrigibly offensive to the residents of the town. A black-and-white photograph of the house accompanied the front-page article. Martin saw his own name captioned beneath the image, and his breath caught for a moment in his throat. In the fuzzy photograph, of substandard resolution, the piece did look horrific, like the scene of a crime.

All publicity was good publicity, he reminded himself. Lying alone in bed, habitually on the right-hand side, he allowed his mind to drift through the possibilities. The art world would surely catch wind of the controversy, and there might be a write-up in one of the monthly publications. The longer the Gregorys resisted, the better for his own career. Perhaps other suburban renegades would contact him about commissions. He felt a sweet shudder at the thought, despite the heavy awareness of the empty space at his left.

Later that week, John Gregory came to the door. He shook Martin's hand firmly, gave a brief, beleaguered smile, and announced that they were going to take the piece down. The battle was exhausting already, and it had only begun. The situation was emotionally depleting for his wife, in particular, who had not taken well to being the town pariah.

They would cover the cost of deinstallation, John said as he rose from the couch. And Martin, naturally, would keep his commission payment. As John spoke, Martin sat quietly and watched his neighbor's gesturing hands, the gold wedding band making designs in the air. He watched the knob in John's throat move up and down the pink column of his neck. When John shook his hand, Martin received the grip impassively. As John left, the front door let in a fragrant breeze before closing with a flatulent sigh.

The following week, a truck came to Martin's house. A man rang his doorbell and asked where they could put the crates. There was no room in the studio—the garage—he told them. He signed a paper and closed the door. He watched through the window as the men unloaded wooden crates onto the driveway. Then the truck pulled away.

Martin stepped outside, and the sunlight hit him flat in the face. He walked, partly blinded, toward the maze of crates on the pavement, each sealed tight. Fingering the perimeter of one lid, he felt the divots where each screw was firmly countersunk. There were at least twenty screws in this one lid. He sat down on the box. The sun was warm on his head, indiscriminately loving. The pale green trees flapped their thousand excitable hands.

He thought of the little pond behind the house, icy in winter, covered with algae in summer. He remembered chasing frogs with the kids, capturing dragonflies. Just now, the water would be clean and cool, nearly pristine. He entertained a vision: a pond bejeweled by insects. Floating grasshoppers and bees, the water shuddering alive. The foam would keep them afloat, and he would go in after them, sink down among them. He would drop through them with his iron weight, completing the piece and bestowing its meaning.

Martin sat for another moment, then used both hands to push himself up. He leaned down to the crate that he'd been sitting on, and tried to lift it, but the strain in his back was too much and he let it drop back to the ground. Straightening, he surveyed the jumble of boxes—too many to count, identical, all equally impossible. He squinted into the sun. A car approached, loud and filled with children. A boy saw him with his boxes and waved. He waved back instinctively. The car rumbled out of earshot, and the small sounds of birds returned.

You're Starting to Get a Reputation

Therese Eiben

Don't look in the mirror. Just brush your teeth and then get in the shower. That's right. Gentle, warm water soothing the old noggin. Nothing to jolt you into the dread.

Don't think about it yet. You need a triple espresso before you do that. Until then, just stick with that numbskull feeling you've got going on. Don't probe it. Don't wonder why *numbskull* is a pejorative term. To you, it's a godsend. If only it lasted.

Even now it's slipping away. Images of yesterday's meeting are filling your head, as if a camera had panned the conference table to remind you of everyone's reaction to you and your big mouth: There's Daniel, the CFO, absorbed with the perfection of his cuticles; Anya, your assistant, mouthing OH, MY GOD at your associate editor, Charles, whose face is, as always, at least when you're around, a marble mask. Ash and Peggy, advertising, openly grinning at one another like it's their lucky day. Kamal, head of circulation, bouncing the eraser end of his pencil on the table, catching it midair. And Margaret, with her blue-black bob, not a hair out of place, gathering her papers, saying, "I'd say that's enough for one day." Look at her. Seamless. Unflappable. She slips out of the room without looking back.

Admit it. This time you went too far. She's going to fire your ass.

So what's the plan?

Call in sick until you figure out a plan.

Dial the general number instead of editorial so the receptionist answers. She's nice, sort of a friend, not that you hang out or anything, but she'd never mock you behind your back.

You say, "Hi," then fake-cough and say, "Hi," again. "Eleanor?"

"Hi," Eleanor says, worry suffusing that one syllable the way only Eleanor can suffuse.

"I'm not feeling well," you say. "It's my . . ." You can't think of what to say; you should have thought it through.

"Contagious?" Eleanor is a bit of a germophobe.

"What?"

"Your . . ."

Brilliant.

"Maybe!" You say, "Maybe I'll be out for a few days, just to be sure. To be safe."

"Riiight," Eleanor says, and the way she says it, you know someone is distracting her.

After a muffled pause as if she has her hand over the mouthpiece, Eleanor says, "Thea, Margaret wants to see you in her office. Ten AM." Another muffled pause and then, "Today."

"Okay," you say, disconnecting the call. You can't even call in sick well.

There are worse things than being fired. Really. And who says

Margaret has grounds, anyway? After all, all you did yesterday was speak your mind. You do that. Well, you blurt, but you often blurt what everyone else is thinking. Like, everyone who has ever worked at *Vox Populi* for more than two minutes knows it's a moribund legacy whose sole purpose is to flatter the aging egos of the board members, seven emeritus professors and retired publishers of twentieth-century literature who oversee a vast endowment bequeathed by an eccentric philanthropist who continues to assert editorial control through the terms of the trust.

"It's time to break the trust!" That's all you said.

Well, that's not all you said. You also suggested that Margaret might be against challenging the trust to protect her $300,000 annual salary. Cue the reaction shots of everyone in the meeting.

You're guessing Daniel had to know what Margaret was pulling down, but no one else on staff would be privy to that information. The only reason you know is that Abelard blabbed it one night when you were both deep into a bottle of Napoleon brandy.

Abelard! Maybe you haven't gone too far after all. You rustle through the obvious, then not-so-obvious places where your phone might be, and once you find it, you disregard multiple unread text and email messages in your rush to find his number, but just as you land on it, you remember how early it is. Abelard would never take a call before noon.

Tick tock. Ten a.m. is fast approaching. You look longingly at your favorite pair of jeans on the floor by your bed, then turn to your closet. There hang five pairs of black Brooks Brothers wash-and-wear slacks, five white oxford-cloth shirts, and two pinstripe blazers, all purchased for you by Margaret on her corporate credit card after it became clear to her that (a) your work as editor pleased the board, which meant specifically the distinguished board chair, Abelard Vartan, and (b) your understanding of suitable work clothing stopped at "not pajamas."

For formal events, you have a Hermès scarf that the board gave you one Christmas. You have no skill at tying scarves (something Margaret could do blind with two broken arms). Most often, you wind up looking like you're about to set sail. Not that you're going to formal events anymore, not since Margaret assigned you to be Susan Sontag's handler at one of *Vox*'s annual fêtes. Margaret usually handles the guest of honor, but Susan S. had a reputation for being difficult, and Margaret wanted to enjoy herself. Margaret can be mean.

Your first task as handler was to get some publicity pictures taken, but when you asked Susan S. to "step this way" for her "photo op," she asked, "In what way is it an opportunity for me?" Not yet fully understanding the disaster the night would become, you gamely said, "I thought that as the author of *On Photography* . . ." and the look Susan S. gave you really took the wind out of your Hermès sail. Once seated, you asked if she had seen any good movies lately, in your mind a nod to her status as film connoisseur. She asked if you knew anything about her beyond her Wikipedia entry.

This made you smile. You knew quite a bit about Susan S.

"I do. I've published several articles about your work and a book review."

"Which book?" Susan S. asked.

"*Under the Volcano*," you said, pleased you'd won her attention.

"I didn't write that."

"Of course you did." You'd spent two months on that review.

"I did not."

Astounded, you smiled at the others around the table, looking for help, looking for any witness to this odd standoff, but they were all busy studying their respective place settings.

"You did," you said.

"Did not," Susan S. said.

"For God's sake, Susan!" You received an ASME nomination for that review.

Behind you a waiter, an aspiring writer—all waitpersons at the fête were aspiring writers—bent down and whispered,

"Malcolm Lowry wrote *Under the Volcano*. Susan S. wrote *The Volcano Lover*."

Of course, you knew that. Your dissertation was on Lowry. It was just momentary aphasia. You turned to explain, but Susan S. had folded her napkin. Susan S. had left.

The waiter leaned down again, asking if you preferred red or white. You said, "Yes." Abelard had to fill in the time slot for the guest of honor speech. Not that he minded. Raconteuring is his favorite sport. You were still drunk at the postmortem confab the next morning. Margaret cut that meeting short too.

Your familiar commute to the office feels solemn. You slow-walk your last moments as editor-in-chief of *Vox Populi*. If you were honest with yourself, which you often are not, you wish you had quit long ago. Of course, you needed the job and the money, but the stress is chronic, and the Brooklynites, as you think of the staff, all a decade or so younger than you (not counting Margaret), seem endowed with more self-confidence and assertiveness than you ever conceived of, much less possessed. They can be mean, too. You found headshots of Susan Sontag signed, *To Thea with love, S.* in your inbox or taped to your desk chair for months after the event.

Abelard says your only problem is self-consciousness, which you wear in public like a rash, and it makes you do and say rash things just to put an end to your excruciating discomfort. Like when you met Edmund White, an author you greatly admire, and slipped him your psychiatrist's appointment card instead of your business card. Or when you introduced Anne Tyler as Ann Beattie. Abelard says you will find your feet in this world. You got married too young—while you and your spouse were both still in school. Academia is nowhere to learn about the real world. You have always been grateful for Abelard's support, his insistence that your future will be bright, but it occurs to you now, as you head toward the firing squad, that you should have remembered that despite being your best friend and most trusted confidant, Abelard is eighty years old. His worldview may no longer apply.

When you arrive, you find Eleanor sobbing, truly sobbing, a bouquet of Kleenex blooming in her hands. This tableau of sorrow sends you shuffling past the glass doors of *Vox Populi*'s offices and into the stairwell to regroup. Could something have happened in the hour since you last spoke? Did Margaret tell her she is firing you? You had no idea you meant so much to Eleanor. Could you have misjudged the rest of the staff? You mentally picture them in one-on-one interactions and in meetings. All you conjure is a slideshow of side-eyes, raised eyebrows, and smirks. Perhaps Eleanor's is a private grief. Maybe her mother has died.

So as not to intrude, you silently turn your key in the door and tiptoe past Eleanor, who is—there's no other word for it—ululating now. You are jealous of her abandon.

Margaret's door is ajar. Bracing for her invulnerability, you square the shoulders of your Brooks Brothers blazer, rap lightly to let her know you are there, and enter. She stands in profile at her desk, her fingertips pressed into the shiny oak veneer, her head bowed, the perfect fall of her hair screening her face. A moment of reflection before she turns to address you. In that moment, you take a deep breath, exhale slowly. The way Margaret expresses anger discombobulates you. You are still hardwired to expect your ex-husband's incandescent rage. Margaret is, by contrast, a cold, proficient assassin. You watch the blood return to her fingertips as she releases them from the desktop. She raises her head, shakes her hair into place, and turns to face you. But instead of her flinty eyes and the thin red line of her lips, you find her, too, crying. Talking softly, kindly, she gestures to the chair across from her desk. She says she is very sorry to tell you that Abelard has died.

You find yourself sitting, not remembering how you got here, only aware of the emptiness filling your head your lungs your heart. Meanwhile Margaret's talking in between dainty blows of her nose. A few words come through the void between your ears: Abelard's heart; the neighbor with a key who found him; his dogs howling and circling his body.

Poor Abelard! He loved his dogs. Over the years, no matter how late it got on the one or two nights a month you hung out with him, exploring the breadth of his knowledge and the depth of his liquor cabinet, he always wobbled out with his whippets—Athos, Porthos, and Aramis—to pour you into a cab. More than once you woke up the next morning laughing at the memory of something he said or did (he had a thing for vaudeville.) Can that much spirit die?

Thump. A percussive noise has been going on the whole time you've been sitting across from Margaret's desk. Thump. She is throwing books into boxes. Her desktop is clear.

Somehow you think she is packing up your belongings. That she has already fired you and you missed that part, which is certainly possible. You often miss the obvious, but you catch up by finding clues at the margins. Subtext. That's why you are a good editor. That's what Abelard said when he introduced you to Margaret, your first boss, your only boss.

The three of you went out a few times at first—you knew Abelard from grad school, where he was teaching a publishing course that extolled a pre–Barnes & Noble, predigital, pre–Title-9–aware book industry. It was 1995. Despite his eminence, not many students signed up, but for you, a man in a crisp white shirt who told witty stories over a couple of drinks felt just like home. Margaret lightened up around Abelard, too, but she didn't drink, and Abelard told you to never trust anyone who didn't drink. It meant they were afraid to laugh at themselves.

Thump. Another book, this one dedicated to her by a famous, no-longer-living novelist.

Margaret has been talking this whole time.

"Sally'll have a first pass of the press release to you by eleven. You need to turn it around so she can get it out by noon," Margaret says, clapping book dust from her hands. "There's a one p.m. interview scheduled with NPR. Lynn Neary."

"Oh, I like her," you say.

"Yes," Margaret says. "She's nice."

Puzzle pieces floating in the back of your head assemble into thought. "Margaret?"

"It seems the board agrees with you. *Vox Populi* is a moldy old publication stuck in the 1950s. And . . ." She pauses to look directly at you and raise one of her microbladed eyebrows, "my compensation package offends them. I guess Abelard had insisted. Anyway, I'm out."

"Margaret, I—" You're about to say you can't possibly do a media interview, but she has walked over to you and now has her hand on your no-longer-squared shoulder.

"I think it was quick, Thea. I don't think he suffered."

She gives your shoulder one awkward pat, steps away to scan her office shelves, takes a final glance at her empty desk, then walks toward the door. Once there, hand poised on the knob, she turns around to look at you, a smile tucked into one corner of her mouth.

"Tell me, Thea. It doesn't matter now. Were you sleeping with him, too?"

Too?

Your face is an open book. From across the room Margaret can read it clearly: initial confusion followed by incredulity and then the heated flush of exposed ignorance. Abelard, whom you loved without fear or question, who knew the squalid details of your marriage and its death throes, who made you—by the exquisiteness of his good company and the fact that he always seemed so happy to be in yours—believe that in time you might regain your self-confidence and get past the fact that your ex had left you for your dissertation adviser, somehow never mentioned that he was having an affair with Margaret.

"Oh, I am sorry, dear." Margaret says. She leaves the door ajar.

You can hear her comfort Eleanor, who, too, has only ever worked for Margaret, and then arrange for her boxes to be delivered to her home. You hear the outer office door open and then lock shut.

Eleanor's voice comes through Margaret's desk-phone speaker. She sounds like a robot with a head cold. "Thea, are you in there? Sally's looking for you."

What were you to him, then? An off-night diversion? The imbalance of your friendship shames you.

"Should I send her in there?" More techno nose-blowing.

You are as hurt as a teenage girl whose best friend never mentioned that she was having sex with your mother.

Someone shoulders open Margaret's door so that it bangs against the wall. It's Daniel, with a box in his arms. You believe for a moment that *he* has packed up your belongings and he's about to tell you to shove off. Then you recognize his framed diplomas jutting out from the jumble in his box, which he drops onto Margaret's desk. "Sally's looking for you," he says.

"What are you doing here?"

"The board has appointed me acting executive director. What are *you* doing here?"

"Good question," you say.

In the outer office, Ash, Peggy, and Kamal form a semicircle in front of Eleanor's desk. They all stop talking when they see you; then Ash and Peggy tell you at the same time—a hint of scolding in their tone—that Sally is looking for you. You nod, remembering the NPR interview, and make your way to your office, each footfall taking you closer to your next public humiliation.

Anya has her back to the doorway, her arms propped on the top of the cubicle wall that separates her desk from Charles's. She is speaking with the animation of good gossip. You hear your name. Anya is ambitious for Charles. She thinks he should have your job.

"Hi," you say, which makes Anya straighten up and turn toward you, then to Charles, and then back to you. Now she clasps her hands at her breastbone and says, like a sorority sister full of fake sincerity, "Poor Abelard."

You nod and make your way to your office, which overlooks their cubicles through a floor-to-ceiling glass wall. Sally's press release is on your desk. Every time your eyes alight on Abelard's name, a thumbtack of hurt pricks a lung. You can't do this. You carry the press release out to Charles-who-should-have-your-job, and you say, "Sally needs this proofed by noon." You glance at the clock. It's already 11:30.

Charles says, "Shouldn't you be the one to do this?" He clears his throat. Anya's eyes are huge and rounded. She wants this showdown. "After all, you knew him so intimately."

Anya can't help it. She gasps. You are known to be a wuss in the face of confrontation, but you discover now that women about to commit public humiliation don't give a damn.

You say, "I think you're confusing me with Margaret."

Anya, who should never play poker, squeals, "You knew? No one thought you knew."

Back in your office, you close the door. There is only one spot—a chair wedged between a filing cabinet and a structural column—where you cannot be seen through the glass wall, where you do not feel like a guppy swimming in an aquarium full of betta fish. You take a seat, try to make yourself smaller so that even someone with her nose pressed against the glass can't spy on you.

Only when you feel a chill on your chest and realize that your Brooks Brothers shirt is wet do you explore your cheeks, which are wet, too. You are crying without any effort or sound, and it surprises you. You thought that after your ex's betrayal you were all cried out. It occurs to you that you might make some notes, at least give yourself a chance of surviving the interview, but somehow that seems foolish now. Maybe you sleep.

Your phone console is buzzing. A disembodied Eleanor says, "Thea. Lynn Neary, line one."

You don't remember why your shirt is damp.

"Th-Thea?" Eleanor, an empath of the first order, fills your name with the dread that normally would be suffusing your conscious mind, but your skull is numb again, and in that narrow sensorium, you rise from your hiding spot and take a seat at your desk just in time to watch the tops of Charles's and Anya's heads disappear below their cubicle walls.

You wipe your eyes with the heels of your hands, can't imagine how wild your hair must look, and then laugh when you remember it's radio.

You pick up the receiver and press the flashing red button.

"Thea Cook?" says a voice.

"Yes," you manage. And then, emboldened, you inquire, "Nynn Leary?" And hearing yourself, you hang up. Impossible. The impossibility of this task.

Your phone buzzes again. Charles and Anya aren't even pretending anymore. Their furrowed brows and critical eyes peer at you over the tops of their cubicle walls.

"Thea?" Eleanor is panicked. "Lynn Neary, line one."

You press the speaker button, not feeling strong enough to hold the receiver. In your mind you hear Abelard say—Abelard, who loved spoonerisms, who would have laughed uproariously had he heard what you just said—"Once more unto the breach, dear friends—" And for a moment you forget how hurt you are and instead remember the night you and he, copper-bottomed pots on your heads, broom and mop aloft, marched around his apartment after several too many drinks, reciting soliloquies from *Henry V*.

"What's that?" Lynn Neary says. You jot her name down and underline the L and the N.

"Oh, sorry," you say. Your mouth is dry. A Sahara. You motion to Anya, tipping an imaginary glass to your mouth. Setting a land-speed record, Anya runs out and returns with a cup of water. She bows, for some reason, as she backs out of your office, leaving your door open. What do you care? How many people listen to NPR?

Lynn, meanwhile, is being very nice. She extends her condolences. She thanks you for taking the time to talk to her on this sad day. She says she believes you have known the literary lion, that's what she calls Abelard—he would have liked that, would have demanded a mane—a long time. You allow that you'd known Abelard for fifteen years. She lists his achievements, his laurels, the history he made in and for literature, then says, "Many people know his biography." She asks if you would share with her some qualities about Abelard Vartan that few people would know?

"Spoonerisms," you blurt, as if telling on yourself.

"Yes?" Lynn Neary asks.

You clear your throat and say, "Words at play. Well, play in general. But, yes, puns."

You clear your throat again, take another sip of water while you ask yourself, Now what? You're going to tell the world that this literary lion loved puns?

"I mean, of course he valued the transformative force of language, its ability to bring audiences to their feet, to tears, to conviction, to conversion, to, um, feel alive."

You stop to heave air into your lungs and to warn yourself that you are speaking faster than your brain is thinking. You have no idea what you'll say next.

"But he also loved the flip side of language. He loved to flip language, to rob it of its meaning. Puns, rhymes. Tongue twisters. Malapropisms. Nabokov. Wilde. Belloc. Ogden Nash. Lewis Carroll. Noël Coward. Gershwin. He could recite all of them. He did recite all of them."

You stop. You are out of breath. You can't go on. Abelard loved Beckett. You go on.

"Play. Verbal. And physical. He said the ability to play was as vital a sign of life as a pulse. If you didn't know how to play, you were dead, dead, dead, Abelard said.

"He could pick up a linen napkin with his bare toes and toss it into the air so that it landed on his head. He told me that was proper etiquette if I ever dropped my napkin at a fancy dinner party." You pause, puzzled about why you said that, then add, "And of course, always take your shoes off under the table when you dine. Just in case."

You take another sip of water.

"Maybe I should stop talking?" you ask Lynn, but Lynn is laughing. She is saying it's a delight to imagine such an august man with a napkin on his head. Before you know it, you tell her how you and he taught yourselves to play the ukulele. You studied old soft-shoe routines on YouTube. Some nights he'd pour a pound of sugar on the kitchen linoleum, and you two would dance, shuffle and slide, his beloved dogs licking their whiskers and snuffling at your heels.

"He loved magic tricks but was terrible at them. Cards fell from his sleeves, quarters rolled on the floor. He knew the whole history of humor, from the ancient Greeks to lightbulb jokes. And nothing amused him more than insults of great wit. Churchill was his favorite, but Shakespeare had a trove."

He made you memorize and declaim them. You remember him shouting, "Louder! Louder! You tell that bastard, Thea. Say it like you mean it!"

And you did. You shouted, "*You are the son and heir of a mongrel bitch*" so loudly that Athos, Porthos, and Aramis skittered out of the room, tails between their legs. And in your own mind, you imagined your ex finally reacting to you. Your ex finally acknowledging your existence, if only to rage at you even more. And you imagined yourself, an independent, individual, sentient human being, standing before him, impervious to his rage.

"Thea?" Lynn asks. "Still there?"

You have been staring at your shoes, cloth slippers you bought in Chinatown, two pair for five dollars. Abelard told you just last week that they were disreputable. This Saturday he was taking you shoe shopping. "To Saks!" he said. "Their shoe department has its own zip code!" You hear him so clearly that you look up, expecting to see him through your glass wall. Instead, you find everyone else, Charles and Anya, each giving you the thumbs-up sign. Daniel is there, leaning against the wall. He is gazing into the middle distance, nodding. Eleanor and Sally are hugging each other and beaming at you. Ash, Peggy, and Kamal have their arms above their heads, like you just scored a goal. On the phone, Lynn Neary asks if you are still on the line. And you tell her, "Yes. Yes, I am."

The Prodigal Daughter

M.G. Stephens

At the time of her mother's death, Eileen had called her once a week from London. She even wrote the odd letter now and then, getting into a correspondence with the old one. They made promises to meet, and her mother reminded Eileen that the old woman was not long for the mortal coil. It was now or never. So, Eileen booked a flight to Dublin and came over one weekday morning in November. Her mother asked Eileen to take her to Clare, where the mother was from, and Eileen agreed, renting a car at the airport before she drove over to Sandymount, where her family's house had been for generations. They packed a small valise with clothes and a lunch basket to sustain them in the journey and lit out of Dublin for the frontiers of the west.

Her mother wanted to go to the usual places a tourist might visit, so it was not so much a sentimental journey to her mother's childhood haunts as it was a trip to the Cliffs of Moher and an afternoon exploring the Burren. The Cliffs were crowded with tourists, even in November, so they purchased a few trinkets from a traveller girl and then went on their way. At the Burren, they lingered much longer, and when the chill wind dug far into them, they sought shelter in the rental car, which was small enough that it almost felt like it might lift off the ground from the force of the wind.

From her handbag, Eileen's mom surprised her daughter with a copy of one of Seamus Heaney's books.

"I didn't know you read poetry," Eileen said.

"There's a lot about me you don't know," her mother said.

Her mother read Eileen a poem about being at the sea in Clare.

After the poem was read, they sat in silence. The Irish were good with their silences. Then her mother cleared her throat.

"It's sentimental," her mother said. "But I like it. I like it the way one likes a greeting card or a popular song that is sentimental."

Eileen listened to the wind whipping around outside. It was as if she were playing Cordelia to her mother's King Lear.

"His later work is sentimental," her mother went on. "It's the early work that counts."

"I didn't know you liked poetry, Mother."

"When you become an OAP, you have to do something with your time. I take the odd class or two, Introduction to Poetry, the Poetry of Ireland, stuff like that. It fills the time."

"Why?" Eileen asked, being a kind of itinerant journalist, poet and philosopher herself.

"I thought it would help me to understand yourself and the work you do."

"Did," Eileen said. "I haven't published a proper book in donkey's years."

"Now, don't spoil the view with a shedful of self-pity, Eileen Elizabeth; there is no need for that out here on the Burren, where we are more pagan than Christian and more two women than a mother and child."

"I'm sorry," Eileen said. "Usually I'm a bit more sanguine."

"You were quite the emotional bundle of goods as a child."

"Don't let's get into me childhood, Ma."

"Luckily I can't remember a thing about it anymore," her mother said.

Eileen set the rental car into drive and moved off. Behind them, the Burren receded; its craggy shore, its colorful weeds, its winds, drifted out of sight in the rearview mirror of the rental car. It looked like it had a million years ago, before history. The only one to age had been Eileen. Her mother looked as she had when Eileen was a girl. Her mother was a woman of perpetual middle age, even in old age. She had her rosy cheeks and disposition, her plaid wool skirt like a third-rate royal, her silk scarf tied around her head and her waterproof overcoat of cotton and synthetic cloth. She wore her sensible shoes. She had been the doctor's wife most of her long life, and then she had been the doctor's widow, a grandmother, an old friend to her neighbors, a church lady, even a writer of left-wing political ideas to the local newspapers. All in all, she was not a bad mam, and that was her life, as she appeared to be at the end of it now.

They spent the evening at a B & B in Ennis. In the early morning, they drove into town so that her mother could attend Mass. They came back afterwards to the B & B and ate a light breakfast before driving back to Dublin that morning, taking turns at the wheel.

As Eileen drove, her mother pointed to the dimpled marks on her daughter's freckled arms.

"What is that?"

"What?"

"Those indentations."

"Tracks," Eileen said.

"Tracks?"

"From shooting up," Eileen told her. Then she said, "I don't know."

"Heroin?"

"For fuck's sake, Ma, I'm fifty-fucking-eight years old."

"You wasted your life with that man," her mother said.

"He's dead."

"I'm at death's doorstep meself, girl. We have to talk. No husband, no children. You're all alone in London. If you collapsed in front of the British Library, people would just step right over you, Eileen. There is no family there, no friends. You are all alone. Isn't it time you came home?"

"For fuck sake, Ma."

"That man took you from your family, your world, for what? To turn you into a drug addict."

"I'm clean now," Eileen said. "That was years ago."

"What did you have in common with a Cuban man?"

"His mother was Irish," Eileen said. "That was the attraction. I reminded him of his mother. That's all men want, they want their mother."

"I was not at all like your father's mother, Eileen Elizabeth."

"Don't kid yourself, Ma."

"Your father loved me for who I was," her mother said.

"Bloody fucking hell," Eileen shouted. "I just missed the turn. Let me concentrate on the driving."

Once Eileen got them back on the right road to Dublin, the car fell silent for a time, and a sort of peace descended upon them. But then Eileen felt the urge to clear the air.

"Santiago was born in Brooklyn," she said. "That's how I became a US citizen too, once we married."

"Did he even love you?"

"He loved me all right," Eileen said. "But love isn't always a blessing."

"I've listened to his music," her mother said. "He was very good at what he did."

Eileen had spent a lifetime away from her family and Ireland. They did not know her anymore. Assumptions had been made about her and then calcified. She was not going to change all that after thirty or forty years with one drive to the west of Ireland or one afternoon on the Burren.

She was clean now and hadn't been high in nearly two decades. She did not want a medal, and yet why didn't they see her progress the way others saw it? The arc of her life now bent towards life and away from the destruction of her addictions, all those years that she and Santiago lived in the Maghreb and travelled the world giving concerts everywhere so long as it was not America.

They had toured Africa many times. She had met Nelson Mandela and Robert Mugabe, to mention two extremes, and they had toured in Russia and the Far East—China, Korea, Japan. They had even gone to North Korea for a concert because Kim Jong-il loved Santa's music.

She had shook the Great Leader's hand, which was soft and girlish and seemed to lack bones. He smelt of strong cologne, with an undercurrent of kimchi.

They had flown from Pyongyang to Beijing, where Santa gave another concert. Then they flew to Tokyo, where he performed for a bunch of VIPs at a sleek, plush hotel in Roppongi. Next, they went to Seoul. After that sold-out concert at the King Sejong Centre, they were approached backstage by some high-ranking State Department officials—two men and a woman.

The woman was a beautiful young Korean American, and Eileen figured her husband would be sleeping with the young official before they left South Korea. It was just the way it was in those days. No one knew he was HIV yet; maybe he was not even inhabiting the virus then. That may have happened later.

The two men had not flirted with Eileen but looked at her disapprovingly. She was wearing a kind of rock-chick velour suit of trousers and jacket in radiant Titian blue, with a ruffly white linen shirt whose buttons seemed to have disappeared in transit. Eileen wore no bra, so what chest she had was almost completely exposed to everyone. Her red hair was like Medusa's, big and curly and flopping about everywhere. Her green eyes rolled around in her head.

She heard the men talking to Santa about revoking his citizenship. For what? he asked. They did not answer.

The younger man wore a tight-fitting dark suit, a white shirt and red tie. His brogues were shined like two black coffins. The older man was a seasoned Asia hand or at least seemed to be one. He was quite tall, towering even over the very tall Eileen, and his face was long and craggy, like the mountains that surrounded the former imperial city they found themselves in. He was a career diplomat, she thought. His suit was dark blue with wide chalk-grey pinstripes; his tie had some college insignia on it from Yale or wherever. The shirt was light blue and button-down, and he wore oxford loafers with bright red socks.

"I was born in America," Santiago said. "I have not broken any laws. Politically I don't see eye to eye with you. But that is not, in and of itself, a crime."

"When is the last time you paid your taxes, sir?" the craggy one asked.

"I stopped paying taxes in response to the Vietnam War."

"That was a long time ago, sir."

"The arc of history is long," Santiago said.

"But it bends towards justice," Eileen chimed in.

"Who's she?" the tall Asia hand asked.

"Wife," Santa said.

"Wife?"

"Yes, that's Eileen Santa there."

Eileen bowed.

Mr. State Department sneered at her.

"Is she an American?"

"You'd have to ask her," Santa said.

"Are you an American, ma'am?"

Eileen smiled at him. She was very high that night.

"I'm asking you a question, ma'am. Are you an American?"

"She's Cathleen ni Houlihan," Santa said, getting into the goof.

There were hundreds of people standing around backstage at the Sejong Centre waiting to meet Santiago Santa, to shake his hand and tell him how much they loved his music. No one could get to him as long as the officials held him captive backstage.

"Ma'am, I've asked you a question several times now. Are you an American?"

Eileen's paleness, even then, was astonishing. There was no one in the room paler than she. She was so floppy it seemed as if she had no muscles to support her long frame. She was not someone, though, who was easily intimidated, and besides, she and Santa had been through the wringer with the US for years. Everywhere they went, spies followed them.

She might look like a wispy pre-Raphaelite portrait, but Eileen Coole was as tough as they got. That was what Santa liked about her. She could handle anything.

"Miss Houlihan, you have the right to remain silent if you wish."

Eileen attempted to speak, but nothing came out. Words betrayed her. She felt the room spinning.

Earlier that day, on the flight from Japan, she had drunk a bottle of Jameson's and topped it off with a lot of marijuana. She did a few lines of cocaine that a stagehand provided her. She also snorted some heroin. The bottle of Irish whiskey had come from Kim Jong-il, who had given it to Santiago as a present. No one but Eileen drank it, and it was long gone by the time the State Department people spoke to them.

Eileen woke up still drunk in her hotel room in downtown Seoul, and then the entourage grabbed a bunch of limos to take them to Kimpo Airport on the outskirts of the city. When Eileen came to again, they were on another 747.

"Where are we going?" she asked one of the technicians who travelled with the group.

Santa was somewhere else on the plane or on another plane, probably with the Korean American woman from the State Department. He might not agree with the official's politics, but that never stopped him from making love to someone.

"We're doing three shows in Manila," the techie said. He was a young guy, a very good sound man. He was bearded and long-haired, like a throwback to the hippie era. His home was around Detroit, where he had been a theatre director. His name was Forest. He had gone to Yale Drama School, and when the tour ended, he planned to open a fringe theatre in Detroit. Eileen slept with him that night. But she remembered almost nothing about it. It was not the first time this had happened with Forest, and it would not be the last.

They were in Manila for two days before Santa showed up a few hours before his first concert. He was high on heroin, reefer and vodka and about as coherent as a snake. But everyone knew the routine, and he played especially well that night. The whole group did, but particularly their leader.

Eileen loved his music and the man, but after the concert she let her other feelings be known to Santa.

"I want a divorce," she said.

"What's this all about?" Santa asked.

"I want it now."

"In Manila?" he asked. "Isn't this a very Catholic country? I don't think they give divorces, even for you, Cathleen ni Houlihan."

"Fuck you, Santa," she said. "Fuck you and the horse you rode in on."

"It was a plane, Eileen. Are you all right?"

A month after Eileen visited her mother, the old woman took ill. One of her brothers called her in London and booked her a flight over to Dublin. He had an intuition that their mother was not going to make it.

Eileen arrived Thursday evening. The next day their mother's cold turned into a wheezy chest and a cough. By Saturday it turned into pneumonia. Sunday she was coherent for a few hours, then lapsed in and out of consciousness. By Monday her mother was dead. Eileen and two of her sisters, Maeve and Fionna, stood vigil around the sickbed, attending to their mother's final wishes. Before the mother expired, she spoke on Sunday morning to them, one sister older than Eileen, the other younger. A fourth sister lived in a cloister in Nova Scotia, Canada, and she was nowhere to be seen, nor would they be able to contact her easily or to fly her home to Dublin if her mother died.

"I'm so proud of all my girls," her mother told the three sisters, who ranged in age from fifty-five to sixty. "But I'm especially proud of Eileen."

"Eileen?" Fionna asked.

"Who?" the younger sister, Maeve, said.

Eileen was speechless.

"What's so special about Eileen?" Fionna demanded.

Fionna had a point. She had cared for their mother almost daily in old age. Maeve was there after work several times a week. They dumped bedpans, ironed sheets, took her for convalescent walks around Sandymount, spoon-fed her porridge, read to her from favorite books. All Eileen had done was to take their mother in her last month of life for a two-day outing to Clare.

Big deal.

"I'm so proud of Eileen," the mother said, "for a million things, including she got herself clean and sober, the first one in the family."

"She's the only one in the family who's an addict, Ma," Maeve deadpanned.

"Eileen went to graduate school in America," her mother went on deliriously, speaking as if Eileen was not there. "She writes poetry, girls. She's a poet."

All of them spoke as if Eileen weren't there.

"For fuck sake," Fionna said.

"I wish you wouldn't talk that way," her mother said.

"Eileen bunked off from her doctoral program in California to shack up with some Cuban criminal who took her halfway around the world."

"That's a lie!" Eileen shouted.

"She's a common whore!" Fionna shouted back.

Their mother coughed.

A nurse came in and scolded them for the tensions they had created around their dying mother's bed.

Their mother wheezed and coughed and went in and out of consciousness from that point onwards, the clarity of her mind slowly oozing out of her tired bones. That was the last of their mother's verbal pyrotechnics. From then on, their mother might wake, even smile, hold a hand, seem to whisper things, but nothing more was said. She never spoke again. The whisperings were false messages from the beyond, sounds upon the wind, birdcalls.

"What about us?" Maeve asked no one. "She had seven children. Eileen's not the only one."

"Look what you've done," Fionna said.

"Me?" Eileen asked.

"You've upset me mam," Fionna said. "We cared for her in old age. Wiping the oatmeal off her chin. Changing her adult nappys. Bathing her. Giving her sponge baths. What did you do, Eileen?"

"She wrote her a poem for Mothering Day," Maeve said.

"That was years ago," the oldest declared.

"It was years ago," Maeve agreed.

"I could have written that poem," Fionna said.

"Then why didn't you?" Eileen asked.

"You beat me to the punch."

They stood over their wheezing, dying mother, arguing with each other like they were children. In a sense, they still were. Each inhabited a space in the family that had been assigned quite early in life. Fionna was the caregiver; Maeve was a kind of afterthought. "The Mistake," her siblings called her.

Eileen had been the prodigal one. She was not like the others—smarter at her studies, more creative, easy in her ways, never struggling in any subjects. She was gifted in many things. Boys adored her, and so did girls at school. Teachers loved her clever answers. She was gifted, they said. By comparison, Fionna had been a figure of fun, slightly overweight, slightly less pretty than her younger sisters. Maeve had been too airy-fairy, not rooted to the earth as Eileen had been. All of them could sing and play the piano, but Eileen had the purest voice and the surest hand on the piano.

Her sisters believed—despite the evidence to the contrary—that Eileen never struggled with anything. Even her rough times in London added to the legend of Eileen Coole.

The sisters—all but the nun in Nova Scotia and Eileen—had married, had children and raised these families, slowly taking them away from their aspirations, whatever they were: singing, dancing, acting, painting. Her brothers were doctors and lawyers, solid citizens of the realm. Her sisters had married well. But none of them did the things of their youth anymore. They did not even attend plays or concerts unless it had something to do with their children's lives.

Prodigal Eileen had gallivanted over the globe, sending them postcards from Egypt or Singapore, calling them every few years from Phnom Penh or Mumbai. She was drunk or high, her speech slurred, and what she said was repetitious and inane.

One Christmas years ago, the family was about to settle down for a dinner, the goose just out of the oven, when Eileen called them from South America. She was with Santiago in Buenos Aires. Did any of them ever see a proper tango? The steak in Argentina was beyond belief, she said. Eileen would say that, though. She was sending some very special soap home to their mother. Be on the lookout for her package. But of course, that was years ago.

"We all can't be Eileens," Fionna said at their mother's death vigil.

"I only want you to be yourself," Eileen told her big sister.

Her baby sister cried at the foot of the bed.

Eileen went over to comfort her, but Maeve pushed her away.

Fionna wet their mother's lips with a sponge. Their mother mouthed words, but nothing was intelligible; nothing was spoken ever again coherently. The unspokenness of death descended upon the hospital room as the sisters dug in for the long night ahead.

Eileen wanted to apologize to her sisters, but she did not know exactly for what, so she hung back.

She went and sat in a chair in the far corner as Fionna sponged their mother's lips again and Maeve cried at the foot of the bed.

Eileen, being the prodigal one, sat in the corner by herself.

Oonark

Elizabeth Altomonte

What she would remember, when she saw the dog thrashing in the Sound and the disarticulated body parts of her husband and daughter trawled up from the wreckage of the Magister, was Oonark. She might have remembered the wedding guests she had stranded, her daughter to be married in the afternoon, with still so much to get settled: the bridesmaids moaning over hems and tightened waistbands, the florist complaining that the lacy overlays did not match the ivory hydrangeas and the event planner unable to find the cash box for the money, for the money—the newlyweds were in their twenties, and they had nothing, after all. And the gin wasn't right, said the bartender, the in-laws wanted Bombay Sapphire and the grandmother swore by Beefeater, what was there to do, what was there to do?

And then her husband demanded one last ride in the air with his daughter, in the Fouga Magister, only hours before the ceremony, before his daughter became another man's. It would be just a little spin, no barrel rolls or Immelmanns, in his Magister; why, he'd only just procured the vintage airplane, and he wasn't sure if the Magister could handle maneuvers such as those. And her daughter said not to worry, the air would do her good, and the dog should come, the dog should come! the dog who loved the roar of the engine and the feel of great speed upon her frame, her majestic leonine great frame.

And after an hour, the call came through, when the bandleader was doing a run-through of the Louis Armstrong song, testing the amplifiers of his sound system. Someone approached her, the reverend, and clasped her hands. She didn't like anyone touching her hands, they were her hands, after all. There must be some dignity left, something left of her, on the day she was to lose her only child, to be wedded. And when the reverend said, Your husband's plane has gone down in the Sound, she thought, Why, such a silly thing to say, *Your husband's plane has gone down in the Sound.*

And before she knew it, a LifeStar helicopter appeared on her meadow, where there was only alfalfa growing before the white pole tent had been erected, and wedding guests who had arrived too early, the kind of friends and relatives who habitually arrived too early, to lend a hand they'd said, when they were only nosy, to be invited to an event such as this! And these guests who had arrived too early were now witness to the monster on the meadow, and they must have thought the helicopter was part of the wedding, part of the elaborate spectacle, until the helicopter ascended from the meadow.

The LifeStar helicopter ferried her to the Sound, because the LifeStar pilot knew her husband, and he thought that with any luck he might be bringing her husband and daughter back, alive, to the hospital. But when they arrived at the Sound, there was only the dog, thrashing, thrashing, in the ocean. It was a strange sight, to see her dog in the ocean, for despite living only an hour from the sea, she could not recall ever seeing her dog in the ocean. And of course, the dog would have taken to the ocean, the dog was a natural swimmer in the ponds and streams and swimming pool on their estate. How strange it was to watch the animal from up above, thrashing, thrashing, while the rescuers fumbled through pieces of the fuselage, pulling out legs and shoes and a torso. She could not fathom how it was possible to burn in the water, while the dog was thrashing, thrashing, the helicopter stirring up the waves, so at times the mammoth dog's head went under. And as the helicopter moved lower to the waters, she saw that the pale fur of the animal was red, and the redness bled into the water, so the dog was thrashing in a red sea, next to a piece of the wing, next to her daughter still strapped into her seat, still smoldering, while the dog thrashed and thrashed.

And then she remembered Oonark, and she looked down again, from the LifeStar helicopter, to see if there were any ice floes, for she had thought of Oonark, Oonark on her ice floe, but there was no ice, only chunks of white foam spewing out from the fire rescue vehicles and Coast Guard ships. But there could have been ice, it was quite late in the season, almost November.

How strange it was to think of Oonark, she had not thought of Oonark for many years, and the last time she had seen Oonark, at the National Gallery of Canada, more than twenty years ago, Oonark had told her of the ice floe and a great ringed seal thrashing in the water. And this was ominous, Oonark had said, a great animal in the sea, for it signaled life, for so many years the great ringed seal had disappeared.

Oonark had told her of the ringed seal at the National Gallery of Canada, at the Commendation Ceremony for Oonark, where Oonark had said, with only minutes to spare before the actual ceremony, "We must see the Rubens," and Oonark takes my hand, too firmly, and again, we return to the Rubens painting, as we have done for three days since the inauguration of *The Hunt* at the National Gallery of Canada, and I tell Oonark that we must hurry, and we walk quickly past Parinaya's *Horse Mounted Tiger Hunter* and George Catlin's *Dying Buffalo Bull in a Snowdrift*, Oonark casting a disdainful eye at the painting of a wounded buffalo, a wounded buffalo whose blood is seeping into the frozen ground while an Indian brave lies motionless, dead, beside the beast, his head-dress and bow scattered around him. And we hasten by the *Puckeridge Foxhounds* and the Flemish hunt scene by Van Der Straet. And we also scurry past *Caribou Meat Covered with Flies* by Janet Kigusiuq, Oonark's daughter, the etching of a dismembered caribou lying on the tundra.

At last, we come upon *The Hippopotamus and Crocodile Hunt* by Rubens, and Oonark dashes toward the painting, positioning her face at the mouth of the hunted crocodile, and a guard rushes up, and I step in, warding him away, for the guard does not know Oonark, the guard sees only a gnarled gnome in braids and brightly colored parka. The guard does not know that this wizened woman is the greatest artist in the history of northern art. And Oonark's nose almost touches the painted linen canvas, and the guard watches intently as Oonark breathes and breathes. I pull Oonark back, and Oonark says the smell of the alligator is powerful. I tell Oonark, once again, that the reptile in Rubens's painting is a crocodile, not an alligator.

I tell Oonark that the alligator belongs to the family *alligatoridae* and the crocodile to the family *crocodylidae*. I tell Oonark to look at the shape of the jaw, at the shape of the nose: alligators have snouts shaped like shovels, and crocodiles have longer, more pointed noses, but Oonark dismisses me with her hand, in the same way she dismissed me during the installation of her wall hanging *Kiviuk and the Grizzly*, when she caught sight of the Rubens painting. "Ah, the alligator!" she said. Oonark had seen such beasts in the *National Geographic* magazines discarded by

Christian missionaries who had once served at Baker Lake. These leviathans were not of her earth, Oonark had said, but of someone else's earth, creatures unbound to ice and snow and winter darkness.

The duty has fallen to me to take care of Oonark during the cocktail hour before the Commendation Ceremony, before Oonark will be appointed as an Officer of the Order of Canada, the honor to be bestowed upon her by Prime Minister Pierre Trudeau. The duty fell to me because I am accustomed to Oonark, because I am a textile artist who was sent to Baker Lake two years ago to set up a printmaking program at the arctic college. But now, with only minutes to spare before the ceremony, Oonark will not leave the exhibition gallery, for she wants to see the painting of the hippopotamus and crocodile once again.

While we stare at the masterpiece of Rubens, the cultural attaché strides into the exhibition salon dressed in a Balenciaga ball gown. The cultural attaché strides up to where we stand and inquires into the meaning of the ruckus, and I whisper that Oonark will not leave. And the cultural attaché asks, "For Christ's sake, why won't Oonark leave?" I report that Oonark will not leave until she understands the painting, which is not entirely accurate. During times such as these, it comes to me why Oonark is sometimes thought of as bullish and ignorant, but such characterizations are off the mark. And because I understand the true nature of Oonark, I tell the cultural attaché to please leave us. "We will come, we will come soon."

So the woman in her finery takes her leave, and I tell Oonark that four hundred or so years ago, when only the nobility and royalty were permitted to hunt, many earls and dukes hunted in exotic lands and captured magnificent creatures such as lions and tigers. And these dukes and earls brought these lions and tigers back to their country manors; the scenes of magnificent beasts were found to be alluring and awe-inspiring. For this reason, Rubens included more than one animal. He included the hippopotamus and the crocodile, and the fierce hunting dogs, so the painting would exude danger and power.

"Look!" I say, pointing to the pelt of a leopard draped across the upper left horseman. "And look at the snake, sliding over the left arm of the fallen hunter, and look at the sharp teeth of the frenzied beasts. Look at the faces of the riders, charging into the midst of the battle. And look at the fallen warrior with his spear raised. Look at the diagonals, how they heighten the sense of movement. And look, Oonark, at the weather! Everything is thunderous, thunderous, the flaring nostrils of the horses, the blowing manes of the horses, and the animals' mouths gaping wide. Isn't it amazing, Oonark?"

But Oonark only smiles and places a finger on her lips and whispers, "I will tell you something later."

We return to the Grand Salon, to the ballroom of moneyed patrons, Oonark wearing her parka and her mukluks, her demeanor one of bored indifference. And James Butler takes the podium to tell the story of Oonark.

Butler begins by saying that Oonark was born within the frozen shelter of a snowhouse, and when she was born, she was not crying, she was just looking. Oonark was just looking, looking, looking at everything. Her given name was Una, which means "this one," before it became Oonark, so even from the day Oonark was born, she was singled out from the others.

When Una was just a girl of twelve, she was married to Quabluanuq, and for thirty years Oonark was married to Quabluanuq. With Quabluanuq she had twelve children, four of whom perished at birth or as small children.

And when Quabluanuq died, Oonark was left alone with eight children to provide for. Oonark filled her stone pots with dried meat and fish, and she secured these pots across the barren, rocky landscapes during the snowless months of summer, for in the winter, food would be scarce.

In the winter, she returned to the seacoast, to the igloos on the frozen waters of Chantry Inlet, where she hunted the ringed seal for food and lamp oil, because she had no rifle to hunt for caribou. And she would fashion the skins of the ringed seal into summer tents and into garments, which she would elaborately embellish for her family.

In time, seven of Oonark's children married and went off, leaving her with one daughter, and then there came a time of great famine, when Oonark was staying in the camp of Quabluanuq's brother, Quinangnaq.

And when Quinangnaq decided to move his camp closer to Baker Lake, his dogs became too weak to transport everyone, and Quinangnaq was forced to leave Oonark and her daughter behind. Quinangnaq hurried to the settlement to get help.

Oonark had little fuel and hardly any food, and the stove malfunctioned. Oonark tried to hunt ptarmigan but was not successful, and she had to leave her daughter in the igloo to seek out food, so they might live. Although she was weak and freezing, Oonark tried to chisel holes in the thickness of the ice, so she might fish, but a piece of ice broke off and Oonark became stranded on an ice floe.

After many days, Oonark was rescued by a corporal in a supply plane; she was near death. The supply plane brought her to Baker Lake, and along the way, the pilot picked up her daughter.

And Oonark and her daughter settled in Baker Lake, where, for a living, Oonark cleaned skins, cooked meals, washed dishes and worked as a janitor at the mission houses. And then one day, when she accompanied her daughter to the settlement school and saw the drawings of the children, Oonark said that if she was given proper materials, she could do better than that. A doctor was visiting the school, Dr. Andrew Macpherson, a biologist who overheard her comment. And Macpherson saw to it that Oonark received sketch pads and felt-tip markers, in order that she might try to draw.

When Macpherson saw her drawings, he sent six of them to the Cape Dorset printmaking shop; Cape Dorset was already a recognized Inuit Art Center. Oonark's prints were released in the Cape Dorset portfolio when Oonark was fifty-four. She was fifty-four when she began her life as an artist. Art collectors in the south recognized the printmaking skills of Oonark, and it was arranged for Oonark to have a workspace of her own and a modest monthly stipend. And Oonark came to visit New York City, where she autographed first-day cachet prints for the United Nations, where hundreds of collectors stood in line to receive her autograph in Eskimo syllabics.

Then, because she was skilled at sewing, Oonark made a parka for William Larmour, of the Department of Northern Affairs, Larmour who was conducting research into the living conditions of the Inuit. The parka was decorated on the cuffs and hem with animals and human figures. Afterward, the delighted Larmour sent Oonark a duffel filled with decorative materials, so that she might experiment, but what he did not know was that Oonark was equally adept at embroidery, so when she took up the pieces of felt and embroidery floss, the wall hangings she produced, of hide and stroud and thread, were no mere crafts but superior pieces of art, one of which would hang in Canada's Legislative Assembly Hall.

While Butler spoke, I looked over at Oonark, who was paying no attention to his words. She was rubbing her hands, for she was suffering from numbness in her callused and swollen hands. Oonark sewed continuously, night and day, and if her fingers became too cramped and pinpricked, she would decorate caribou skin clothing with colored strips of fur, beads, musk-ox hair, animal teeth and sometimes long black strands of her own hair, which she would laugh at but would leave bound into the sewing.

She sewed while sitting on her narrow cot, inside her one-room house, a dwelling called a matchbox, or a coffin box, because it was so small. And because Jack Butler had encouraged Oonark to make her wall hangings on a gargantuan scale, she fashioned them as a scribe does his scroll, working only on that portion which rested in her lap, her sewing materials spread out all around her, never seeing her work until it was completed. Because she never worked beyond what she could see, her hangings were episodic, made of fields and borders and repeated patterns.

I was there when Oonark put the finishing touches on the wall hanging known as *Dream of the Bird Woman*, and together we opened up the work, which was twelve by nineteen feet, longer than her house. When it was unfurled, it seemed incomprehensible that Oonark could have envisioned the larger composition without seeing the fabric surface in its entirety.

I would sit alongside Oonark on her cot, both of us appliquéing, and when I told Oonark that she should rest, she said all she knew to do in life was work, all she knew in life was that she was old and lonely, and the work gave her something constructive to do.

I never asked Oonark why she did not remarry, for among her people it was regarded as unheard-of for an older woman to live alone. It was not for lack of suitors, for many men came calling at her door, but Oonark was not concerned if she was regarded as a curiosity.

I was a good companion for Oonark, and she would sometimes inquire into the situation of my own life, what work my hands would be doing when I was her age. I shrugged and told her that most likely I would marry, have children and a dog and a property near the Sound, and the talents of my younger years would be subjugated to projects at my children's schools or to volunteer undertakings. My textile work would never, in all likelihood, see the gallery light. And Oonark would scold me and say, "Such a story!"

After months and months of working beside Oonark, I began to notice many things in her work, like how she placed women in the center, women dressed in various arctic garments, with birds and animals atop their heads or birds and animals perched across their shoulders or within their reach, but such things were difficult to translate because Oonark talked in circles, and Oonark worked in circles.

She would fashion a rabbit, then little rabbit droppings, and the droppings would become the tail, and the tail would be fastened to the rabbit. In another drawing, the tail would become heart shapes, and then the heart shapes would be transformed into an elaborate border pattern, fastened to the rabbits, and then the border pattern fastened to the rabbits would slowly suggest the profile of a woman's face. And if you looked closely at the woman's face, it would look like a rabbit, so that everything was a circle, in a circle, but Oonark never thought of things this way. Her work was just her work.

After the Commendation Ceremony was completed, when the distinguished guests began their dining, Oonark beckoned for me to follow her. I did not ask where we would be heading; I knew it was to the crocodile and hippopotamus painting, for Oonark wished to tell me something.

When we drew near to Rubens's *Hippopotamus and Crocodile Hunt*, Oonark declared, "The polar bear could take them all." I was surprised to hear such a childish thought, for this was not the intention of the painting, to decide which beast was mightier than the other.

Then Oonark told me of the ice floe, Oonark told me that when she was on the ice floe, far, far away from her daughter, who was alone and starving, the winds were howling, and she dreamed of plump red sea trout and the summer eggs of snow owl and the succulent haunches of fattened caribou. And when she no longer had the strength to dream, a great ringed seal appeared at the jagged edges of the ice floe, and the ringed seal was thrashing, thrashing, in the water.

And then a polar bear appeared behind the seal, and the mouth of the polar bear opened wide, and Oonark saw the great beast's teeth and blackened tongue. She was frightened, and the hair stood up on her neck, but Oonark studied all the movements of the great white bear until she was no longer frightened. And the polar bear bellowed and rose up before her, and Oonark bellowed, too, and lifted up her harpoon, preparing herself for combat. Then the great white polar bear retreated, and the ringed seal thrashed around before her, its dark head bobbing up and down, and down and up.

When I asked Oonark what her story meant, she said I should never inquire into the meaning of a story. She did not concern herself with solving riddles. Oonark smiled and told me that sometimes a ringed seal thrashing in the water means only a ringed seal thrashing in the water. The animal might have been running from something, or fishing, or playing, or the animal might have just been thrashing in the water, for no other reason. Oonark said I must be content with not understanding. Snow melts and becomes part of the air, and part of everything, so it is not possible to find meanings and explanations in experiences. Everything is connected, everything melts and becomes part of the air, and these unseen forces govern every aspect of our lives, from birth to death, from death to birth. And Oonark said that real art is in the writing of her name upon the snow.

These things which Oonark spoke of I did not understand until later, not until decades later, not until I was the woman looking downward at the wreckage of the Fouga Magister from onboard a LifeStar helicopter, a woman who would one day find a piece of that which she had lost when, years after the accident, she would sit upon her bed, her dog beside her, and pick up her needle and embroidery floss and pieces of stroud cut into the shapes of a man, an airplane, a pole tent, and a girl dressed in white.

And when these woolen pieces were assembled onto the fabric canvas and the construction was found to hold some semblance of meaning, the woman would again take up her scissors, and she would cut out the shape of a great ringed seal that looked as if it might be thrashing, or perhaps playing, in the water.

A Quiet Pilgrimage to Every Last Ruined Saint

Gabrielle Hovendon

We meet throwing rocks at the Shkola 837, and right away I know we'll be friends. Zhivka has a terrible overhand but an angry set to her jaw that makes me step back and watch. A stone sails whitely through the air and connects with glass, and then she goes for another. The window shatters. We're thirteen years old, artists in the making. Failure running through our lives like a rotted thread.

We become inseparable almost immediately. We break into peasants' gardens and climb the black cherry trees to shake down handfuls of fruit. We walk past the Shkola 837 and smell the sharp fumes of paint wafting out and assure ourselves that we're not jealous, not even a little. We run half-feral through the streets, and we make plans to start our own studios and art schools. We may have been born into shit, but we won't stay here forever.

This is Spasyavane: grim housing blocks, metal factories and highways that sling around mountains toward nowhere in particular. We grow up surrounded by broken glass and concrete, and we hardly know how much we've been cheated. Our parents work in the factories or they sell cigarettes and prepaid phones in the corner stores or else they drive to the next gray city and work at vague government posts, and at night they come home and fill the hallways with the blue tick of television.

Not Zhivka and me. We're going to make it out. We're dreaming of our first masterpieces because there's nothing else to dream of. Growing up in Spasyavane, we need no prophets to tell us the odds against us. Our home lives are disasters, and this is no place for miracles, but we are not going to be like these other people. She is going to be a painter and I am going to be a woodworker, and together we will become famous.

Before Zhivka, I know nothing about art. I've read instruction manuals and made clumsy pipes and crooked hairbrushes; I've stumbled blindly through projects, chisels in hand. On unlucky days when my father brings me to church with his red handprint still on my face, I sit in the pew with hot blood sliding between my teeth and commit the manuals to memory. The basic dovetail joint consists of the flared tails and the slender pins, *Confiteor Deo omnipotenti, istis Sanctis et omnibus Sanctis*, once properly constructed, the dovetail cannot be twisted or racked or destroyed except by fire.

With Zhivka by my side, I learn how to be an artist. I begin to read about woodworkers, and I pin the pictures of famous works to the wall above my bed at home. We take ideas and spend hours pulling them apart like orange pith. I begin to consider pieces of wood as stories and start unlocking abstract shapes within them. I wear my hair long over my eyes and spend all my time arguing about form and function.

She teaches me to steal bent hammers and chisels from the scrap heap behind the Shkola 837 and smuggle them home under my jacket. She lives with her grandmother in a single room in Block 6, where she lets me keep my tools under her bed. She doesn't ask questions about my black eyes, so I don't ask questions about her parents: Who are they and where have they gone? Sometimes your father is a sadist and sometimes he's a holy bastard and sometimes he's poisoned by the state and it is never, ever wise to ask too many questions.

Fourteen years old. Zhivka makes me pose nude for a painting.

Not like that, she says. I just want to study you.

I take off my clothes, and she folds them and places them on the ground. Her grandmother is out on a weekly walk with the baker's widow, the bricklayer's widow; everyone in this town is either widowed or widowing, and Block 6 is cool and quiet. I lie down on the bed.

Move your arm, she says. I do. I've learned everything I know about painting from watching Zhivka. She scavenges old canvases and brushes from the garbage behind the art school and scrapes the dried paint off the palettes and mixes her own pigments in margarine tubs. She makes an easel out of a broken chair and barters portraits of the local families for balls of wool and blackberry canes and beeswax.

She has a merciless stare, and when she turns it on me, I freeze. I am an object to be painted, I'm a shoe or a fish or a messy collection of lines. It doesn't matter if I'm shy or turned on or embarrassed; it doesn't matter. I am not fourteen, and I am not Sasho.

Her lips purse while she paints. She studies me, and I study all her little unconscious tics: the squinting, the palette held up to the light, the tip of her tongue poked out of her mouth. She is looking into me or through me or near me, and I feel like something laid out for sale, I feel limp and shining and new and remade.

This is my first time being part of a painting, but it's Zhivka's hundredth or thousandth. She makes portraits of everyone she comes across: Dead Gregory, the local farmer who everyone says has died no fewer than five times; the beggar woman in the doorway of the abandoned train depot; the drunk grabbing his crotch outside Sveti Nikola; a neighbor with eleven children; a white cat with six toes.

After she finishes my portrait, she won't let me see it.

Before her, I didn't know anything else existed.

We're different in all the little ways. I'm constantly nicking myself with the chisels, little wedges of pain that rise up all day long. She has a certain dark poise, and when she searches for the best light in the room, I want to stop everything and watch her. When we work, shavings of conversation curl and fall between us.

Have you seen the brush I was—

How do you think this would—

What if I—

I live for the hours I can escape to Zhivka's apartment. At home, my father measures my mother's skirt hems and puts on black gloves when he beats her in order to hide the blood. He's memorized every word of the Eucharistic liturgy, and he knows how to choke with exacting pressure. I carry fury with me like a small knot.

I hate my name because it's his name, too, and I toy with changing it—Boyko, Zlatan, Lazar—until Zhivka brushes my hair behind my ears with her fingertips, murmurs, Sasho, Sasho, don't let him get to you, don't give him any power. Sometimes we try on pseudonyms like new clothes. She'll be the famous Sofia Abadjiev, and I'll be Vlado the Magnificent. We're barely teenagers, and already we feel eternal.

We have a morbid curiosity, Zhivka and I. We sit in the stairwell of Block 6 and smoke cigarette butts we find on the sidewalk and trade tales of heretical artists who had their hands nailed to their tables or their eyelids sewn shut. We wonder aloud what it would feel like. Zhivka describes the blood, and there is just so much of it. We can hardly see for all the smoke we're making.

At the end of the year we both drop out of school. My mother, in her quiet, protective ways, can't make my father send me to the Shkola 837, but she manages to find me an apprenticeship with a carpenter who lives nearby, and my father allows it, just. If the patron saint of forced silence existed, if he had a shrine in our house, he'd take up every inch of available space and overflow into the street.

In the mornings I stand at the cold tap and wash away my plans of rocking chairs and cuckoo clocks and cabinets with secret drawers. Then I go across the street and up into the small space that smells of pickled fish to sweep floors, sharpen chisels, gouge ten thousand tiny triangles into ugly pine boards and learn to be an apprentice.

Zhivka stays home. She does the cooking and the washing and rubs salve into her grandmother's arthritic joints. When the old woman is snoring in bed we go out to the hallway and whisper what we're going to do when we're famous.

The carpenter, Anastas, turns out to be a drunk and a crook but not a bad teacher. At night I reread the pages of my grandfather's woodworking manual until they begin to fray and fall apart.

I make a box with crooked hinges. I make a set of spoons. I learn how to saw curves, and I try my first jigsaw puzzle.

It looks like dog puke, Zhivka says.

We exist, clumsy, raw, swigging stolen rakia. We've always fought, but now our words start to draw blood. We fight like psychopaths. We fight like broke-ass boxers on a losing streak. We read each other's futures in our palms, faces so close our breath tickles the skin. We've known each other for two years, and we still haven't figured out if we're in love or not.

Walking past the park where the drunks and the half-feral dogs sleep. Making complicated plans to run away to the city and see what the real artists are doing, get to the raw nerve of culture where everything important happens. We go down to the oily river and watch the ships moor and unmoor, and our hearts are gypsies and whores, and we almost never touch.

In July we both turn sixteen. On the night before my birthday, we wait until our houses are quiet. We sneak out and take the little winding lanes behind the peasants' houses to the base of the Kamaka. We have blankets and a flask of rakia, and we are going to the top of the mountain to watch the stars jitter across the sky. We are going to the top of the mountain to push ourselves to the breaking point.

The trail is dark, and we're pretending not to be scared. Our voices are too loud for the black woods, but we're arguing anyway, fighting about art school, and for the hundredth time I'm saying it's a waste of time, and for the hundredth time Zhivka is saying she needs it to make connections. Neither of us is saying what we're really talking about.

We walk, and the honeysuckle clutches at our ankles. Our voices are full of night-speak, grandiose arguments and vulnerabilities. When we finally get to the overlook, we're holding hands, all our fighting used up. It's a cloudless night, and all of Spasyavane's streetlights are too far away to ruin the mood. We watch a few bright cars weave through the streets, and I feel more luminous than the entire ruined city.

From here it's a few short steps to losing our virginity. We spread out the blanket. We drink the rakia. I bend to kiss her, and our teeth bump and draw blood. We are reckless and ready for nothing.

The next week she announces she's taking a vow of chastity.

For my work, she explains.

It's nothing personal, she adds.

She starts painting the icons in August, and by St. Bruno's Day she's mastered them. She reads long, moldy books, and her lips move soundlessly over the ancient words as her fingers trace the old-story saints. Their pictures are flat and not moving, and they stare through dead white eyes. Their halos are gold and wafer-flat. She paints them all, the lesser holy men, the Old Testament prophets and patriarchs, the evangelists, archangels and apostles.

She spends eight, ten hours on them every day. For the first time, she doesn't tell me what she's doing, and she doesn't ask for advice. I watch her out of the corner of my eye, the thin washes of brighter color and the masturbatory little brush strokes, around and around on each saint's creamy skin. There is white gesso on her fingertips and propolis coating her fingernails.

I am partly to blame. She uses terms I don't recognize, "ske-lion" and "first flesh," and I don't interrupt to ask what she's talking about. I grind the red clay for her liquid bole and bring the animal glue myself. When she's gilding she won't let me into the room.

If you breathe too hard you'll blow away the gold leaf, she says.

This new silence between us is thick and unyielding, but I keep helping her. After her paintings finish curing, I'm the one who applies the warm linseed oil. I'm the one who cuts and sands the poplar boards for the paintings. I'm the one who does every-thing, who can't seem to stop.

At home I drift between monotony and terror. Here's the thing: life can be mostly fine, months of peace and quiet, but what you'll remember is still the thirty seconds with your hand held to the burner. My father allows the carpentry apprenticeship except on the days he doesn't, and then it's pain and lectures and punishment until it seems like even my own future is nonnego-tiable to me.

Anastas receives a commission to replace the rotting pews in a church in Spasyavane's old quarter, so I start spending long days away from home. I fetch tools and record measurements in front of an altar draped with a brittle froth of lace. Sometimes Zhivka comes by to watch me work, to watch the old women gibbering their prayers in front of the icons, and Anastas elbows me in the ribs and grins. The air is stale; the church's icons are illuminated by hundreds of candles burning thin and yellow as witches' fingers, candles that burn before each saint in tarnished holders and jelly jars and old bottles of baby formula. I can't understand why she would want *more* of this.

Everything's complicated, she tells me. She's painting more than ever, and she still won't show me anything she's working on. She writes long letters to faraway artists and famous painters, people she's never met. When I confront her, she throws a tube of phthalo blue at my head.

It's always everything and it's always complicated.

I start sleeping on her floor. I fall asleep while she's painting and wake up with her still at the easel. She tells me I have nightmares, that I cry out in my sleep, but I don't believe her. In dreams we are all right. In dreams we are happy together, we hold hands and have pet names, our spines dance and tangle in electricity and everything we say is holy—but then in dreams we are different people.

Awake, we tear into each other worse than ever. She says she loves me. She says she's going to kill me if I don't stop leaving sawdust on the floor. I tell her she's a fraud and a hack. I call her a stubborn lunatic bitch. I tell her she should stop worshiping those shriveled-up saints and she tells me everyone worships something. I have nothing to say to that, but the truth is on the tip of my tongue.

You, I think. *You, you, you. It's always you.*

One morning I wake up and find her on the floor next to me, her head cradled against the curve of my hip. If life consisted of only these tiny shards and nothing more, I think, I might almost be happy.

When she wakes up, she teaches me how to apply gilt. Bend down to your bench and breathe onto the red clay. Smooth the gold leaf onto the water from your lungs. In the cool morning air you'll add layers and layers, and after a few hours you can burnish the leaf to a high glow. In the meantime, you sit and bicker, and you wonder if this is a love story or a war.

Wait for the few thin molecules to adhere. Wait for luck.

In May it begins.

They appear nailed to telephone poles and propped against doorsteps and wedged between crates of potatoes and carrots at the bodegas. They appear in the old style, flat-faced and done in dull gold, expressionless, draped in olives, browns and reds. They are the church's saints, exquisitely painted, and there is something hideously wrong with all of them.

They weep blood, or they have two heads and spikes protrude from their shoulders. They are dead and rotting, lolling tongues the color of fish bellies. They have patchy beards, bones show through their skin, and their sores are abscessing. They can't even save themselves.

The patron saint of cigarette butts: grinning down from its lamppost with yellowed skin and smoker's teeth.

The patron saint of broken accordions: weeping dusty tears over the doorway of the defunct sheet-music factory.

The patron saint of tampon applicators, serene and bloody with a tangle of white cotton strings dangling from her outstretched hands.

The patron saints of fallen acrobats, alleyway abortions, inoperable cataracts.

What the fuck, I say to Zhivka. I know they're hers the same way I know her eyes and her voice and her hands are hers. What is this supposed to mean? I ask.

But she isn't explaining anything.

That summer Anastas is hired to restore a state official's mansion, and I can numb my feelings with work. There's so much crumbling and decay in the mansion that some of the Shkola 837 students are hired as well. We get to know each other around the whine of the saws, and I start taking cheap bottles of slivova out to the fields with them after work. I show some of my sculptures to the carpentry girls in their black jeans and spiked boots, and they coo over my work and caress the pieces with blunt fingers. When I kiss them they taste like ash. They are warm and fast-moving under my hands, and when I smell their sweat and shampoo I miss Zhivka even more.

She is still painting. The patron saint of hand soap. The patron saint of bar stools. The patron saints of fish heads and dirty cowards.

The people of Spasyavane are outraged. The priests are apoplectic. At home, my father rages and wonders why the city doesn't take down the blasphemous work, but the saints are bolted to walls or perched too high to remove without ladders, so they stay and preside over us all. When I can't sleep I go out and smoke cigarettes and walk their routes, a quiet pilgrimage to every last ruined saint, and I feel Zhivka's absence like a knife in my side.

We sleep together only once more that entire summer. It's on an aching blue night in June when her grandmother is out and we're feeling restless in our skin. The whole concrete city is singing to us. We are young, and we might as well fuck this one up right. Afterward we lie staring at opposite walls, and I know she is keeping something from me, she is holding something just out of sight, and it is more than a handful of perverse saints, and it may just ruin us.

I build a bookshelf. I build a table. I carve a set of Christmas ornaments, and I save up the money I earn running errands for Anastas and slave over a pair of mahogany bracelets for Zhivka but then don't give them to her.

I veer surreal. I make complicated little sculptures for my father's noonday anger, my mother's smooth calm, the grandmother and her aged cadre of widows. Zhivka is still making saints, and I will not do it, I will not worship, I will make wickedness instead.

That summer, I carve trespasses of the flesh and of the mind. I carve small abstract tortured shapes. I don't tell Zhivka what I'm doing, and she doesn't ask. I carve the sin of secrecy. The sin of lust. The sin of artistic delusion. I carve and carve, and I find that if I'm lucky, for a few hours I can disappear from myself altogether.

This is how we fall apart:

First there is the acceptance letter, crisp and congratulatory.

Then there are Zhivka's explanations, none of them reassuring. This is what the saints were for. I was afraid you would persuade me not to do it. The capital isn't really so far away. We'll visit each other all the time.

Lastly there is my blind madness, which comes over me like something white and liquid. I tear her apartment open and find the art school essays folded under a shawl in the closet, and I read them, every last word.

All I want is a place away from here, she's written. *All I want is somewhere to do my work.*

The next day I come and collect all my tools from her apartment. I don't speak to her for the rest of the month. By the time I come around and offer to help her pack, it's too late. The school year is starting, and then she's gone.

For the first three months, Spasyavane goes on without her, and I don't. She is gone, and I am still here. She is learning to paint masterpieces, and I am five hundred miles away from the only person I ever cared about. She is a deserter; I am the soldier too dumb to follow suit.

No one else seems to notice she's gone, but I mourn enough for the entire city. I cut my hair and stop eating. I burn the only painting she ever gave me, a tiny watercolor of a hill. Weeks of rage and sadness. Weeks spent dragging myself around like a rabbit with a broken leg. I've been hit and I've been stabbed and I've been thrown down stairs, but this is something deeper, a wound I can't get to.

This is fucking bullshit.

Every morning on my way to work I pass the patron saint of lost foragers. I look at him on his telephone pole, hair tangled and eyes wide, bloody scratches on his cheeks. He looks back at me, and I don't know who pities whom more. At night I come home silent and aching and I can't bring myself to say her name.

Zhivka writes me letters. She's found a place to live. She's doing well in school. The other students are amateurs, dilettantes who paint icons with crooked noses, too-big heads, spotted vestments and catawampus eyes. She's become friends with the carpenters who supply the school with poplar boards and frames, and they all say her talent is once in a lifetime.

They're nothing like you, she writes.

My father's fury at my haircut and black clothes and moodiness is nothing compared to what happens when he finds my sin sculptures. Without Zhivka's room to hide them in, they've overflowed my closet and piled up on the floor next to my bed. I'm not sure what makes me keep carving them, but I can't seem to stop: the sin of selfishness and the sin of wishing ill for a friend and the sin of desperate masturbation and just throwing love away like a rag.

My father's disgust is clear, but for once it does not frighten me. When he calls me a godless child, I tell him to go fuck himself and all his holy anger, and I hit him with a clean uppercut that leaves my knuckles ringing; then I walk out of my house for good.

I borrow money from Anastas, empty my wallet and rent a tiny studio above a liquor store. I cobble together a collection of used rasps and handsaws and set up a cot behind my workbench. I wake up every morning with sawdust in my hair.

I don't know how to fix myself, so I dive into my work. I borrow a scrollsaw and learn inlay and marquetry. I make a clock and a chess-board. I make more clocks. Jewelry boxes. A set of candlesticks. By the time Zhivka finishes her first semester, I've started getting commissions.

Winter drags on. The work keeps coming in, both in Spasyavane and in nearby cities. I come home to my studio with money in my pockets and hold long, elaborate arguments with the air. I'm twenty pounds thinner, and my gums bleed on and off for weeks. I lock myself in my room and destroy the door and the better part of the walls. I horrify myself with the thought that I'm turning into my father.

Spring, and the earth unclenches itself. The fruit trees begin to flower, and a spray of color washes over the bare branches. Zhivka's letters have been dwindling for weeks, and when they finally stop coming I realize I've been waiting six months for her to appear in my doorway.

No more.

I find her in a rented room in the Marinov ghetto. The capital center is bright and gleaming, but the buildings out here are made of scabrous concrete, and their addresses are spray-painted on the doors. All I can think is, she escaped Spasyavane to come to this?

Inside, someone is shouting down the hall. The ceiling is brown from rainwater. When Zhivka answers the door, her eyes are dull and her hair is long and lank. Her clavicle looks like it could crumble into dust. She stands in the center of the room, folds her arms across her chest and tells me I can't stay. She has on a dirty smock, and there is paint tracked across the floor and dried in her braids. Stacked against all the walls are canvases stretching, canvases curing. Everywhere I look: canvases.

The rest of the apartment is only four walls. There's no furniture, just a chair, some Sternos and a ratty nest of blankets on the floor. She's been living like this all year, she tells me.

There is a sweet whiff of opiates and decay on her breath. Her voice has no bite to it, and when she tells me to leave a second time, she's really asking what took me so long.

We stand side by side, skeletons with broken, crooked hearts.

Oh, Sasho, she says. I've seen such incredible things.

Then we slide to the floor and sit there in the clutter of paintings. She murmurs into my shoulder, and I comb the color from her hair and tell her I know. In the whole long ragged history of our country, there's never been anything quite like us.

Listen: We are no role models. Tomorrow we'll wake up and fight. Tomorrow we'll shout at each other until the landlord has to be called. She'll call me a liar and I'll call her a thief, and we'll get drunk and laugh and cry and generally bring out the worst in each other, we perverse creatures. What else can we do? We each fashion our own escapes, rickety things made of wood and paint and string and hope, and when the dust settles we live with what is left and are made new, saints of nothing but ourselves.

The Pickers

Ernest J. Finney

SCOTT & EDWARDS, ANTIQUES, PAINTINGS, PRINTS, FURNITURE, ORIENTAL RUGS, SILVER, PORCELAIN, BOOKS. She stepped back a little so the receptionist could see who she was and buzz her in. AUCTIONS, ESTATES, APPRAISALS. It was like being admitted into a fantasy world. Anything was possible in this building. The receptionist, still on the phone, nodded her back through the second security door to Bernard's office. She was a minute or so early for her appointment. "And what do we have today, Tracy?" She could hear the usual sneer in his voice, as if her being there at all was somehow laughable.

She took her time unlocking her briefcase and then arranging the five drawings, each in its archival sleeve, on his desk. Bernard was good; he didn't lean forward: moving just his eyes, he studied each sketch in turn. He didn't break a smile. Too stunned at what he was seeing? The expert on twentieth-century art. They had been playing at this for the last sixteen years.

It had taken all her nerve to walk into this place that first time, when she was twenty years old. She hadn't established herself yet. No, hadn't defined herself yet; that was more accurate. Worse, she hadn't understood it was just another game with pages of rules that got more complicated as the years went on. That what happened between Bernard and Mrs. Scott and herself would keep changing as the risks increased, so none of them could predict the pattern of the next encounter. But with all their knowledge and experience and degrees, they were still sitting ducks. And the best part was they wouldn't let themselves understand that.

Bernard's office was as huge as most living rooms, one wall covered with framed degrees and awards and photos, another with shelves filled with books, porcelain, and carvings. She had not tried to imitate this decor, rich people's decor, in her town house. What their own homes were like she couldn't imagine.

"Tracy, I'll have to check these out, of course."

"Be my guest. I'll give you until this Friday; today is Tuesday. I have an appointment to show them to someone else on Saturday. And I'll need a receipt. That's right. Just write on my pad here," and she spelled the name to piss him off. "A-m-e-d-e-o M-o-d-i-g-l-i-a-n-i, five sketches. Now sign it and date it. Very good, Bernard." She picked up her briefcase and walked out.

What a surge of strength she felt, reaching the street. She could lift their building up by one corner, given the right grip. And it wasn't just her CDs and investments that made her feel rich, powerful. Though why was she still doing this, if not for the money? Because she was clever? For more money? She had to admit she wasn't sure. She'd only allowed herself the challenge of engaging with Mrs. Scott half-a-dozen times. No, this was the eighth time: once every two years.

Later that morning, unsettled, she stopped by her mother's new place. These visits were always by whim, never from a sense of duty. Her mother's current shop, one of a dozen or so through the years, was in a half-filled strip mall between a Chinese buffet and a beauty salon. Wheeled racks of clothes lined the sidewalk out front. A group of kitchen chairs, red vinyl, patched with duct tape. A trike, a plastic rocking horse. Her mother knew her customers. She'd been ashamed to be seen in any of her mother's places when she was a kid. But she'd had no choice but to work there then.

Her mother, slim as ever, hair dyed carrot orange this time, was watching her though one of the pristine front windows: she cleaned them herself with vinegar and crumpled newspapers. The shop lights were out to save on the cost of electricity. HIDDEN TREASURES was on a newly painted sign; all her shops were named that.

"Got anything good?" she called to her mother from the doorway. They never hugged or touched if it could be avoided.

"Everything is good," her mother responded as always, without cracking a smile. The walls were covered with hand-painted plates, would-be Indian artifacts, plaster ornaments, scenic photos, and amateur oil paintings. There were shelves of cookie jars, salt and pepper shakers, brass figures, mugs. Lighting fixtures and faux glass chandeliers hung from the ceiling. On the floor, every type of furniture from sofas to porch swings. The merchandise was packed so tight the store felt like the inside of a moving van, desks on top of tables and chairs on top of the desks. For a dealer like her mother, a sizable stock meant prosperity. Gaining salable items was the hardest part of the business. Her mother watched her look the place over.

"You've been buying storage lots?"

"When I've had the money. People are bidding too high; maybe the recession really is over."

Storage lots: a quick way to acquire goods. When people didn't pay their fees, their unit contents were sold at auction. They were chancy buys, but you could triple your money if you had patience like her mother, plus enough of a clientele to turn the stuff over fast. There were no previews; you never knew what you were getting. The thought got Tracy's blood moving faster.

Her mother looked her over but didn't mention her weight. Never had. The only time it was ever a factor was when she'd bring over an exercise bike for her mother to sell. Three times now. She'd get tired of looking at them in her bedroom. But she always bought a new one. She had one now, more elaborate than ever. Her mother must be thinking the same thing, because she was taking a look out the window toward her car.

"Do you want a marshmallow, Tracy?" Her mother's one vice now. She lifted the lid to the gallon plastic container filled to the brim with small multicolored marshmallows. Her mother took a fistful and threw them one at a time to the back of her throat. If anyone should never have been a mother, it was this woman. Like she herself should never have been a daughter to anyone. Where did that leave the two of them? With enough sense not to see each other very often. It'd been a year?

She chose three green marshmallows. Why had she come here? Not to do battle, like with Bernard or Mrs. Scott. To uncover some hidden secret? That this woman wasn't her mother after all? Maybe to remember the time her mother had phoned her PO when she was fifteen and yelled, "Come and get Tracy; she's doped to the gills," and she'd done three months in rehab? Or when she'd thrown her out of the house in the middle of the night after an argument, when she was four months pregnant. Or, when she miscarried at six months, "Just as well, Tracy; you can barely take care of yourself." She wasn't getting angry now. It was just habit, feeling the welts of the scars to see how far she'd come.

A car drove up. An older man got out and went around and opened the trunk. He stood there looking down into it, his hand on his hip, as if he expected someone to appear. Her mother took another handful of marshmallows and went out for a look. All the pickers knew where her mother's new place was. So did old customers. The last time she'd come by, one had remembered her from when she was a girl. "Tracy!" the woman had exclaimed.

It wasn't true that the parents' past was their children's future, but at sixteen, pregnant, going from garage sale to garage sale, sometimes a hundred on a weekend, she'd thought she *was* her mother. Following the long lists in the newspapers, crossing each out in turn, taking load after load back to her mother's store. She got so good she could just stop at the curb and decide if it was worth getting out of the car. After school on weekdays, she toured the Salvation Armys and Goodwills and other thrift shops trying to find the odd item worth more than she would have to pay for it. She was able to survive that way, for a while. Her mother had offered her a percentage of the goods she brought in and a place to stay. But no advice: she'd known better.

On the wall by the cash register, like a lucky first dollar taken in, her mother had hung the framed drawing she'd done when she was thirteen or fourteen; it had been in the place of honor in all the shops. The glass distorted the lines. It was the two of them, sitting at a table, facing each other. Simple. By then she knew it was sketching that she was good at. Pencil or ink on white paper. She didn't like color; it confused things. By the time she got to high school she was doing elaborate scenes: city streets, buildings. Figures. Landscapes. But that was it. She never got any better, never found a different way to approach what she saw. Never took some next step that would change the direction she was going.

Outside, her mother was talking to the picker, discussing price. His cardboard box was filled with old-time kitchen utensils: potato mashers, rolling pins, eggbeaters, a green glass lemon juicer, wooden ladles, and spoons. Money went from her mother's apron pocket—one of those faded cotton wraparounds almost like a dress that she'd always worn as her disguise, just like she wore her own double chins, thick body, fat ass—into the man's palm. The picker came inside and put the box by the door. "See you next time, Dora." It always came as a surprise that her mother had a name that others knew and used.

She'd stopped asking about her father once she reached nine or ten. If her mother knew who it was, she wouldn't say. Only, "I wanted a daughter, someone to keep me company." Her mother had been past thirty when she was born. She'd never asked her how she'd gotten into the business, either. Her mother's father had been some kind of doctor in Ohio; he'd died in 1982 just after she was born. Sad stories have no endings. It was her mother's pride that had kept them off welfare, but it had been close at times. Hand to mouth. Driving around to estate sales on a Sunday, making a buy and then reselling it at an antique store to pay for gas and lunch. Sleeping in the car, parked on some safe residential street, watching the lights go off in the houses as people went to bed, her mother silent in the front seat. The sound of a screw-top bottle of port wine being opened.

Two women came in. "Do you have any dolls?" one asked. She flipped on the lights so they could see better as her mother led them to the back of the store, and then sat down in her mother's chair, near the cash register and behind the glass case that served as a counter. It was loaded on top with old newspapers and magazines and books on collecting and filled inside with things you couldn't see very clearly because of the jumble: jewelry, watches, cast-iron toys, forks, and knives sticking out of coffee cans. Her mother had always subscribed to the theory of disarray, the lure of dishevelment. The proprietor is not aware of her goods, it implied. You can find anything in the mess of this place. The owner does not know what she's got and does not know its true worth: a terrible mistake to make about her mother.

Her cell phone rang. It was Mrs. Scott, setting the time for their Friday appointment and mentioning in passing in her sweetest voice that they'd be joined by some art history professor, an authority on Modigliani, who was examining the sketches. "The more the merrier," she told Mrs. Scott. At one time the woman had terrified her. She'd seemed to know everything. She was the great-granddaughter of the founder of the firm, which still had offices in London and Amsterdam, and a legend in her own right: a bibliophile, an authority on Elizabethan broadsheets who'd written a book on the subject, according to that article in the *LA Times*. That's what had brought her to Scott and Edwards in Pasadena with her first find. Mrs. Scott must have been in her forties then but had looked much younger, skin like whipped cream against her lime-green suit. Pearls. Her hair was smooth and blonde, and her lips were a little swollen, as if they'd been stung by a bee. One look at the woman and she'd almost bolted, that first time.

She began to feel panicked when Mrs. Scott hung up, as if she'd forgotten something. But what? She'd learned how to use panic, as she'd learned how to use happiness. She'd learned how to be less than happy; that was important. Less than happy. A feeling that most people wanted to avoid? Not her. She'd dismissed the goal of happiness as ridiculous. Not that she wanted to feel miserable. But the absence of happiness was a strength. Just rejecting the seeking of happiness, rejecting it when it came by, that was the key. She took three more marshmallows and then a handful, popping them in her mouth like pills.

Her mother reappeared in the front of the store as two pickers came in, a husband and wife, inspecting each item as if their eyes were snapping photos. The myth of hidden treasure was alive and well. That's why Mrs. Scott still allowed special pickers to bring items to the store, through the back door, of course, for appraisals. That's how she'd got in the first time, clutching her book, a first edition, Walt Whitman's *Leaves of Grass*. She'd just read that interview with the director of Scott and Edwards in the *Times*. The book she'd found in an outbuilding on a dairy near Sacramento, hundreds of boxes of old books, left by some long-dead relative. The roof had leaked; a lot were damaged. Some of the books were spoiled altogether, mildewed, green and white spots of mold, and some were warped and swollen. It had taken four days to find a book that she could sell. Then another week to do the research to understand what she had found. That was also an important phase, tracking down the details, the investigation, reviewing it all to see if the treasure could meet her expectations. Oh, boy, she'd thought, was she going to make a killing. But she deserved success. She'd worked hard, sixteen-hour days, seven days a week, sometimes, once she'd understood that, like her mother, this was what she was going to do. She didn't mind comparing herself to her mother. There was something compelling about searching for something that wasn't there. Not knowing what you could find next. The only rule was to never collect anything yourself. Never. Sell everything. Her town house looked like the inside of an empty refrigerator. All glass, white porcelain, and stainless steel. No sign of a collectible.

You didn't have to be an expert on every subject; you could learn as you went along. The people who had the treasure would tell you. So you asked, as you wandered around some suburban estate sale or garage sale, looking at the mounds of clothes, the *Readers' Digest* condensed books, particleboard furniture, the worst junk. "Somebody in the family has died? You've come all the way from Indiana to sell off everything, plus the house?" Looks like my uncle was a pack rat, they'd say. The clues were in the goods. Anything foreign. Anything out of the ordinary. The photo albums. The person taking the money was usually the boss. "What a wonderful collection of stuff. Your grandparents? I guess that was the generation that saved everything. From the photos it looks like he was in the army. A teacher? I've never seen so many books on Egyptian art. He was a doctor? She was in the diplomatic corps?"

Then she asked the key question. "Is there anything else?" Everyone always held back something, maybe because they didn't know how much they should ask for it, maybe out of sentiment. "I can make you a special offer. Anything?"

How many times had it paid off? There was some old sterling; they hadn't a clue what it was worth. A box full of Nazi decorations and daggers. An oil painting given in payment by a patient. "My aunt was an Egyptologist"—and there was a cigar box full of coins and blue stone bugs inside a cupboard. "My great-grandfather taught at Bowdoin and collected old poetry books." Walt Whitman's *Leaves of Grass*, first edition.

Her first presentation to Mrs. Scott was the most challenging and the most nerve-wracking. She filled the small back appraisal room with her explanations. "This first edition has spent the last ninety years in a bank vault. It is in mint condition. There is an inscription in pencil on the flyleaf. It's possible that it is to one of his lovers." Mrs. Scott lifted the cover a second time, then let it fall and slid the book a little away from her, toward the corner of the desk. "You have such a pretty face, dear. You should lose some weight."

She hadn't known what to answer, became more flustered. She'd only weighed 150 then. Mrs. Scott glanced at her watch. "Because this is our first transaction, dear, the first of many, I hope, I can allow you forty-seven hundred."

It was worth more a lot more; she knew it was, but it was like being mesmerized by a snake. She could only nod. Accept the check that Mrs. Scott wrote then and there and slid across the desk to her. Watch the woman rise, lift the book carefully from the desk, and leave the room.

She had followed the book, tracking the notices in the paper until the auction, where it went for fifty-three thousand. The buyer had been enthralled by the inscription. It was a valuable lesson. There were pickers who said that when they came across an exceptional item something like a bell would ring inside them, alerting them. What she had was better than a ringading going off in her chest: it was the ability to recognize the full potential of an item's value, the something else that could make it more interesting or more beautiful.

The two pickers left without buying anything. Her mother brought the doll collectors back to the cash register and rang up the sale, taking the time to write out a receipt for them, although a pickup truck had pulled up outside and the driver, a woman, was standing by the tailgate, waiting. The doll collectors were trading smiles, signaling with their eyes what a bargain they'd got: her mother, with probably 700 percent profit, was stone-faced. But in her own way, her mother was as honest as the day was long. She never sold anything under false pretenses. Sterling was solid silver and plate was plate; oak was all oak, not veneer. She couldn't lie about something like that.

A few times when she was growing up, they'd lived well. Rented a house, had a store in a good location, a two-year-old station wagon. She had piano lessons. Friends who slept over. It was like they were different people. Then when she was fourteen it all changed again. And she changed her own life even more, all by herself. It wasn't just sex and drugs; it was her consistency in exploring personally every stupid act that a teenager could commit. Always making the wrong choices, again and again. Getting pregnant at sixteen wasn't her greatest folly.

Her mother went outside, leaned over the side of the pickup, and looked—a long, long time, for her.

"Tracy, come out and see these." Her mother wouldn't be doing this unless the goods were too rich for her customers. "This is my daughter," her mother said to the woman. They exchanged nods. There was a trunk, a couple of wooden chests, something else, and before she could examine it, the woman said, "An old English writing box. Victorian." With *Antiques Roadshow*, the whole world had become knowledgeable. *Antiques Carnival*, it should be. A joke, pure and simple.

Two chests, a trunk, and the writing box. Her mother kept up the patter, how bad business was this quarter, giving Tracy the leisure to look. The first chest, a turn-of-the-century carpenter's toolbox, red fir under the green paint, dovetailed. The trunk, barrel top, embossed tin over wood, lift-out drawer. Leather handles broken on the ends. The second chest was interesting: pine, the joinery a type she hadn't seen before, the lumber hand planed. The exterior had been stripped and then stained and varnished, for a coffee table, probably. The hardware was brass and handmade. Inside, a metal holder for something. A knife? A sailor's sea chest. Oh, my, who would have thought? The picker was trying not to watch her, she saw, but couldn't help herself.

If she had a specialty, it was furniture. She'd lived for a time with a furniture maker who used only hand tools. Jack could do anything with wood. The best part was going around looking for hardwood, cutting up a black walnut with a two-man saw out in some farmer's orchard that had just been yanked up. One time back then she'd asked her mother if she was ever happy. "Once in a while," she'd said. But Jack was always happy. You couldn't get him down. They'd lived together for almost three years before she'd walked out. He'd asked her to marry him, her only proposal. It wasn't enough. Happiness wasn't enough. But it was a sweet time.

Sometimes she thought of pickers as supplicants. Not herself, not her mother. This woman, though. It was an apt label. How desperate was the supplicant? She couldn't guess but would find out. Being fat was the same as dressing poor, the way her mother did every morning: no one took you seriously until you wanted them to by mentioning money. The picker was telling her mother that she worked in a convalescent home. The perfect place to acquire items.

"What's the lowest you'll take?" she asked the woman.

"Nineteen hundred for everything."

Her mother began scolding the supplicant. "Why in the world did you ever stop here? My customers can't afford this kind of stuff."

Like jumping rope in elementary school, she skipped in. "I was thinking more of three hundred for the two chests. I'm not interested in the trunk or the writing box." It was like being a girl again, dickering. Her mother yanked out her pocket calculator and pressed in some numbers as if she were a CPA, then shook her head hard, like she was banging it against a wall. An adamant nine hundred dollars from the picker. Her mother calculated again, sighing.

"Mother, I've got to go." She opened her purse, counted out three one hundred bills and a twenty. "Here," she said, holding out the money, and the picker grabbed it. Her mother moved fast, opening the tailgate and sliding the chests onto the sidewalk before any of them could change their minds. Once the picker had left, they loaded the chests into her car. Then they went back inside the store. She could tell her mother wanted to know. "The smallest is a nineteenth-century seaman's chest; there's a standing offer that starts at five thousand for one at the Maritime Museum. This one was handmade on a ship, I think."

"Why not the writing box?

"It's a replica. They're still manufacturing them. I saw them in the Baltic last summer when I bought all those Russian icons. Lithuania."

Her mother looked interested. "Do I get a finder's fee out of it?" Then she giggled, a girlish, unnerving sound.

"The check's in the mail," she said.

Her mother, always a better actress than she was, picked up the newspaper and started looking at the classifieds. Silence had never bothered either of them, but for some reason she couldn't shake the image that had jumped into her mind when she said the word *check*. She'd forged her mother's signature on enough checks to make it a felony. "You're going down this time," the assistant DA had promised her when she was twenty. But her mother had intervened, to her surprise. "Will you pay me back, Tracy?" She'd nodded. A month later she'd found the *Leaves of Grass* and had the cash. But to this day, she'd never repaid the money.

"Oh, I forgot," her mother said and started rummaging around the counter. "I know you like them too." Her mother bought at the big box stores; she held out a bag of marshmallows half the size of a pillow. How had her mother got that into her head? She had never especially liked them as a kid.

"Well, thank you," she said as two girls came in. She looked at her watch and was surprised to see she'd been in the shop over two hours. Her mother was talking with the girls, who wanted some old *Life* magazines for a school report. "But I won't sell them to you unless you promise to list them as sources in your bibliography," she told them. Her mother wasn't dumb; she'd had a couple years of state college. The girls took her seriously. "I promise," one said before they left.

"I have to be on my way," she told her mother, getting up in a rush to escape. Too obvious, she knew.

"Don't forget your marshmallows." Her mother handed her the pack. Both made sure their hands didn't touch.

Her appointment with Mrs. Scott was at three. As she'd expected, both the museum curator and the art history professor from the university were there with Bernard and Mrs. Scott and the company attorney, all sitting at ease around the trestle table that had come from a monastery in Le Marche. The men stood up as she entered, and Mrs. Scott said, "Good to see you, dear." She shook the men's outstretched hands and took the empty seat at one end of the table.

"Well, Tracy," Mrs. Scott said. "You never cease to surprise us. We have just a few questions about attribution and provenance. Bernard?"

"That you found these sketches at a Buenos Aires flea market sounds improbable enough to be true, Tracy, but please develop the scenario a little more for us."

She'd been expecting that. "The Eastern Bloc countries are grasping the capitalist system way too fast for me, so the last couple of years I've been roaming in South America, where a lot of the national economies are in shambles. In Argentina in particular, after the economic crash, a huge percentage of the former middle class now lives in poverty. As you can imagine, Bernard, this means there are lots of interesting items surfacing."

They were listening like little kids at story hour in the public library. People like these enjoyed narratives of enterprising fieldwork.

"In BA there's a Sunday open-air antiques market out in the San Telmo district. I had been there before, but I usually spend my time with selected dealers or shops that I've dealt with in the past. Busloads of tourists hit Plaza Dorrego every Sunday; the aisles between booths are jammed; tango dancers, mimes, and musicians are all out in full force; it's a madhouse. For some reason, I went again. I got tired after a while and sat down on some brick steps. Next to me was a booth that specialized in hats, everything from brass firemen's helmets to Borsalinos. But there was a box stacked with sheet music too. I started looking through the music, and then there were some graphics and then the sketches. . . ." She paused there.

"Attribution . . . well, everyone knows the portrait stories, of course." It was the art history professor. "There's certainly no dearth of research verifying their authenticity." He was lecturing. "I've personally interviewed an extraordinary gentleman, still alive, though very old, whose family came by one during that critical period in Paris. That Modigliani did sketches in bars for drinks, there and at the cafe Chez Rosalie for dinners, is beyond question. And these examples are exceptional. But what I don't understand is how these four different sketches of four different people were found together in the same place."

"I think that could be easily explained," Bernard said, "by assuming their initial purchase as a set by a collector. And it could have been that the four were members of a family group that Modigliani encountered one night. All are signed; the signature has been authenticated. The paper has been tested."

"And how did they get to Argentina? That is my question," the curator said.

It was Mrs. Scott who answered. "As you probably know, the patterns of immigration to that country didn't peak at the turn of the century but continued into the fifties, refugees and others fleeing the aftermath of the Second World War. Nearly all came from Europe. Forty percent of the current population has Italian blood. Plus, from the turn of the century until the '70s, there was an enormously affluent upper class."

It was interesting that both Scott and Bernard were defending her. This had never happened before. The more doubt cast on an item, the lower the price they had to pay for it.

The professor took off on a long anecdote about the artist's wife, who at nineteen, nine months pregnant, jumped out a second-story window a day after Modigliani's funeral, killing herself and unborn child and leaving another daughter, who became an art historian in France, with whom he, the professor, had spoken once at a luncheon.

Mrs. Scott interrupted. "Tracy, we have an auction scheduled for the spring, a major work of Modigliani. An oil of Beatrice Hastings, the English woman he lived with for a while. The sketches will sweeten the sale."

It was warm in the room. She could feel the whole weight of her body as if she were holding it up with her forefinger above the table. "We want to buy the sketches from you."

The silence went on too long before Bernard said, after glancing down at a sheet of paper in front of him, "For eight hundred seventy-seven thousand." Everyone at the table was watching her.

Something was wrong, but she didn't understand what. "For which one?" she asked, not cracking a smile.

"For all of them," Bernard said.

She could have six times that if she could find the right collector.

"The provenance for these drawings leaves a lot to be desired," the attorney said.

She looked at her watch, stood up, and slowly started gathering the drawings. Mrs. Scott stood up too. "Tracy?"

"No. I gave you first refusal, and you never made a serious offer." She walked out.

When she was eight her mother had come into some money, her share of a sale of property after someone in the family died. Her mother was a believer in her own dream, which was to own a shop with a good line of antiques. She was always attending workshops and subscribing to magazines, *Smithsonian* among them. She decided they should drive out to Washington, DC, and go to the museums. It was probably the only time she could remember that her mother was really relaxed, no money worries.

They spent a whole week and went to a lot of museums. In one of them, a painter with an easel was copying a still life—dead rabbits and birds—that hung on the wall. She watched, standing behind him, for a long time. He was there the next day too. You couldn't tell the difference between the two paintings. They were exactly the same. At another museum, a whole room was full of high school kids sketching from paintings, their teacher going around to look at their work.

It was a couple of years before she tried to make a copy of someone else's drawing herself. It was harder to make a copy than to draw an original. It had to be exactly the same or it wouldn't work. At school she won awards. Most teachers hadn't realized she was making copies. And she stayed with the line drawings. They suited her.

Then, at fourteen, it was like someone had padlocked her brain and left the lock dangling on her forehead: the rest of her body took over with its own agenda. She still drew, but it was like therapy, trying to go back to another time. There was no returning.

There were a number of e-mails the next morning from both Bernard and Mrs. Scott, each one with a better offer. She'd think about them later: she was too sick now. She'd woken up sick, in terrible pain. At first, she thought it was a heart attack. Then she knew it was her gallbladder; a doctor had warned her a few years back, but she knew better, hadn't seen an MD since then. She'd overeaten the night before, plus a dozen doughnuts for dessert and then the whole bag of marshmallows while she worked at her drawing board on the plans for her dream house on the property she'd bought up on the north coast near Gualala.

She stayed sick. She stopped eating. The first day wasn't so hard because she felt so bad; the second because she was still full. But the third and fourth days were awful—headaches, bad breath. She rode her exercise bike. She'd gone on diets before, but this time she just stopped eating altogether, sipped water or unsweetened grapefruit juice. The fifth day she drove around town just to get out of the house. Coming back, parking in her garage, she made herself look at the pine seaman's chest in the backseat of her car. One time in some national forest she and Jack had found a downed ponderosa pine that had been struck by lightning. A big tree. Jack was ecstatic, scrambling through big sections of heartwood scattered like some giant's woodpile, as if he'd found a diamond mine. "It's already kiln dried," he'd yelled.

She unloaded the chest and the toolbox she'd bought at her mother's and put them into her storage unit next to the other things—a hand-carved wooden mannequin, a drop-leaf desk, cherry under the gray paint, a walnut headboard—all from her mother's store.

That evening she read the e-mails from Mrs. Scott again. Then again.

She knew. All this time, starting with *Leaves of Grass*, the woman knew. Like the old joke about that brushfire in the Hollywood Hills when thirty-seven authenticated Van Gogh sunflowers went up in smoke. Like the famous Berenson: his percentage of the sale price was way higher when he was able to authenticate a painting than when its provenance remained unclear. What would anyone do? What would she do? What would her mother do? She'd been using Mrs. Scott and Mrs. Scott had been using her. All those years she'd thought she was so smart.

She had thrown out her bathroom scale years ago. She went out and bought a new one. She didn't want to depress herself by finding out her current weight but kept the scale ready for some future date. She started eating a can of tuna twice a day and a bowl of oatmeal for breakfast. If she'd used her extra weight as armor, protective covering, what would she expose herself to without it? She'd be out in the open, revealed.

The e-mails from Mrs. Scott stopped, but the FedEx man kept knocking at her door nearly every morning. Suspicious people started parking across from her building at odd times, just sitting in their cars. She went out only at night. She rode her exercise bike thirteen hundred miles the second month. She realized she couldn't just pedal away from her life. But she wasn't ready to face it, either.

One night, wearing just her sweats, going the back way to the convenience store, she saw Bernard out front, talking on his iPhone. He looked right past her as if she weren't there. He didn't recognize her? She'd cut her hair and dyed it blonde. She went into the store and bought a dozen cans of the water-packed tuna she lived on now. But he was waiting for her outside. "Tracy? Is that you? I knew you had to come out sometime. We'll give you whatever you want for the drawings."

"I don't have them anymore." She was ready with her follow-up answers: I sold them to a private collector. He wants to remain anonymous. Or, They were stolen from me.

"Find some more, then. Go back to Argentina and bring some back."

Bernard had known all that time too.

"That's not possible. I've left the antique business."

He laughed. "You have an obligation to us, Tracy. We brought you along. We have done business with you over the years, and we want to continue. You're being unfair. Don't do something that we'll all regret."

She was unfair to them? Her whole life had been unfair. She became indignant. "Tell Mrs. Scott that it's over." The word *unfair* was like a kick in the stomach. She turned to walk away. Unfair? Unfair? When she got to the corner he yelled after her, "It's not over until we say so."

She ran up the steps to her town house, got inside, and bolted the door. Unfair. She'd thought she was so smart. Every two years, confirming her own cleverness. She remembered once taking a signature of President William Harding into Mrs. Scott. "That's very nice, dear, but it's much better if the signature is at the end of a letter; it's more salable. President Harding was such a philanderer; he must have written his mistresses from time to time." A year and a half later she'd come up with a note from President McKinley to his ailing wife. How had she forgotten this? Somewhere in her head she had to have understood that they knew.

An old scene came to mind that hadn't appeared for years. After she got pregnant, the district had sent her to a special school for kids who either had a child or were going to have one: you could take your baby to the nursery there while you were in class. School was only in the morning, and afterward all of them waited outside the school for the city bus, putting their books and the babies down on the lawn by the bus stop, smoking and talking—most babies were in plastic carriers; a couple were just on their blankets—and when the bus came, they'd all hop on. One time they got on the bus and a whisper went around: "Tiffany left her baby." No one tried to stop the bus; no one yelled or nudged the girl. They all watched out the back window as the baby on a white flannel blanket faded away in the distance like an abandoned newspaper.

For nights after, she'd had bad dreams: dogs finding the baby, or a devil-worshipping cult sacrificing it on an altar. In reality, a school librarian found the baby and it was returned to its fourteen-year-old mother, but something a lot worse happened later. She didn't allow herself to remember what she'd read in the paper a couple of years later about Tiffany. But she'd understood even then that the baby, like Tiffany and herself and her mother, would never get to use up much of the happiness allotted. That it was useless even to try.

She got the drawings from where they were hidden in a big atlas. Lit the right front gas burner and took each drawing out of its cover and watched the flame spread across the paper. At the last inch she dropped each one in the sink. She had found the drawing pad in the pile of sheet music at the booth in San Telmo, stamped *Fabriqué en France 1923*, every page blank. The figures were originals out of her head, in Modigliani's style.

All those years she'd believed she could become different from everyone else, that the thousands of clicks of adjustment she'd made would transform her into another person, even though the changes never seemed to survive self-examination. But she was the same. She and her mother were the same unhappy person, getting by the best they could. She'd betrayed her mother and herself. For years. That part she couldn't change.

Kristin's Uncle Otto

Kerry Hardie

Yesterday I sat at this window and took Kristin's book in my hands. The courier's van had gone back down the road; the packaging lay scattered on the floor.

Irish Artists in Their Studios: Photographs by Kristin Larsen.

A statement, a book to be left around on display, the title itself an assertion: out there exists a sect whose exceptional lives may be glimpsed in its pages.

I opened it at the index, thumbed down the list till I found my own entry, turned to the relevant page. I looked at myself. Long sweater, dark boots, baggy, paint-stained trousers. One of my hands holds a brush, the other rests casually on my left hip. Behind my right shoulder, the high window floods the end of the studio with last spring's clean light. Kristin had knelt for the shot. Because of the foreshortening, my hands seem larger than my face and have more presence. I am looking slightly downwards, into her camera. Most of the subjects have chosen head-and-shoulder poses. Even those who have gone for three-quarter-length have diluted the statement by sitting or kneeling. Only my photo is this uncompromising. I am wearing no make-up, and my dark hair helmets my face. The caption over the photo says my name is Eilish Lynch. It gives my date of birth, then a long dash to show that my date of death has yet to be recorded. It says I am a painter.

I sat looking at my face for a long time, wondering who lived behind it. Who was the "me" I called myself? Not a healthy thought, this. Too much introspection, not enough being. Time for the garden.

So, I closed the book and put it on the table beside the half-smoked packet of Major and the empty coffee mug. No ashtray. I go outside to smoke.

The Holy Guild of Artists. Once I'd believed in the sect, would have sold myself, body and bones, for a promise that someday I'd feature in just such a publication.

And here I was, included, courtesy of Kristin, Kristin's Leica, Kristin's international reputation. She chose me for this publication, insisted I was of the elite.

The book itself was a commission from an independent body called Aiséirí, a new initiative set up in Dublin to argue that the arts will save our international reputation, boost tourism, salvage the tattered remnants of our image round the world.

And art sales, like everything else, have suffered badly since the crash.

You can imagine the conversation:

"A show. New York if we can get it. Photos—easy to access, easy to ship. Irish artists in their studios, working away, undaunted. And a book—large format—something tasteful, something for embassies

and E.U. presentations, visiting finance ministers, the IMF. . . . We have to shift the bank-and-property-bubble fallout, rebrand as the land of saints-and-soul . . . ."

"We'll need an international reputation—"

So they'd talked to a man in the Arts Council who'd given them a list of names—

And Kristin had said yes, she'd be interested, but she wanted a say in the selection of the artists.

A silence down the line. She'd offered them a cut rate, and they'd hummed and hawed a bit and then agreed to deal. They'd do half the selection; she'd get to choose the rest.

I'm a painter—quite a good one—so she put me on the list. Then she rang to tell me all about it. That was eighteen months ago.

I was struggling with an overgrown border when Sarah's phone call came. Spring was already galloping ahead. I was heaving out my favourite perennials, pulling them free of the worst of the weeds and dumping them in a heap on the mossy grass. Once this was done, I'd break off anything that was salvageable, heel it into some corner, weed-kill the jungle, then replant. Blitz gardening. I didn't approve of myself, but the scutch grass and vetch had woven themselves in round the roots. I should have done it years ago. Dug the whole lot out, begun again.

The mobile rang. I fumbled around in my mud-stiffened gloves, but I couldn't get hold of the phone before it went onto message. I mostly don't bother to listen to voice mail, but somehow the arrival of Kristin's book the day before had thrown my balance. I needed the sound of a human voice, despite the peace of the garden.

Which was why I keyed in 171 without a glance at the number. Then listened to the furious voice of my sister Sarah.

Sarah hadn't phoned me since she'd gone to America. Fifteen years. I sat down on the grass beside a heap of bearded irises. My body felt as though it was having an electric shock.

Mechanically, I started into snapping off the outer tubers. I know this sounds dysfunctional, but it's how I cope with pain: do something slowly and carefully, preferably with something alive that you'll spoil or kill if you make a wrong move. And it has to be something I do with my hands, something to ground the thoughts, stop them from whizzing around in my head in an endless loop.

The exposed bits of the tubers were pale gold, like the ginger-root I use when I'm baking fish. Kristin used to cook fish, but it always went straight into the pan. Buy fish, throw in frying pan, eat with bread. Sometimes she fried the bread, too. Fish-fried-bread. Horrible. Once I'd asked her if they ate it like that in Norway, and she'd grinned and waved a piece round on the end of her fork, offering me a bite. She hadn't answered the question; her mouth was too full. Sometimes she ate boiled spinach as well, and there was always porridge when she was suddenly hungry and there was nothing else in the press. She didn't care much about food, but she needed to eat to keep going. She'd rather have lived on coffee and cigarettes.

After a while I got up from the grass and dumped the iris discards into the barrow. So far my pain therapy didn't seem to be working. I'd intended starting in on the geraniums, but suddenly they seemed too like Sarah. Blue and showy and ruthless survivors. My hands were shaking so hard it was no use trying to prick out seedlings. First Kristin's book, then Sarah. I'd switched off the phone, but getting rid of their presences was harder.

I'd been deeply in love with Kristin, though I'd never told her. That was years ago, back in our student days in Dublin, when Michael and I were both in our final year at the National College of Art and Design and Kristin had wangled a part-time lectureship at Dun Laoghaire College of Art. She wasn't interested in teaching; she just wanted to be in Ireland so she could learn a different light.

She had a room in Monkstown—a big, bare, light-filled Georgian drawing room on the second floor, half furnished with the bare necessities. She paid no rent—she knew the man who had the flat, a cameraman from Trondheim, where she came from. He was away somewhere in Africa—something to do with poverty and drought. There was no lease; it was all friends of friends, and anyway the floorboards were precarious with dry rot. Someday it would be gutted, renovated and sold on. In the meantime Kristin used his bathroom as a darkroom, and if she wanted a wash, she stood in a basin of water on the kitchen floor.

Michael and I shared a single room in a warehouse not far from NCAD. It wasn't really a room; it was more just a big empty space we both lived in. As far as the landlord knew, we were only using it for a studio, but there didn't seem to be any sense in paying out rent, so we'd scrounged a couple of mattresses and settled in. Someone gave us one of those minicookers you used to see in bedsits, and Michael was resourceful when it came to running in cables. There was a tap and a sink and plenty of light from high windows and skylights. No frills, but we had the essentials, plus friends who had baths and hot water.

Outsiders thought we were lovers, but close friends knew better. The arrangement suited us both. Michael liked company when he was working. He wanted someone to talk things through with, even though he didn't always like what I said. And he'd given me the camouflage I'd needed in those days. Or thought I did. Maybe I didn't—but if you think you need something, you probably still do. I'm not certain Michael knew how I felt about women because I never spelled it out. I'm still stunned that I somehow resisted the urge to confide in him, even when we were getting drunk together, taking off our undergarments, showing each other our most intimate thoughts and aspirations.

The other day an American woman in a class I was teaching asked me what a shift was. She'd been reading a book about Synge and the *Playboy*— all that business of the riots in the Abbey Theatre on account of the word "shift." It was an archaism that had fallen out of use, I said. It meant an undergarment, something intimate that touched the skin.

Afterwards I wondered if it was the origin of the modern expression "to shift," meaning "to get off" with someone or, more accurately, to get your hands on them, as Sarah got her hands on Michael under Kristin's nose. I never got my hands on Kristin, but perhaps I never really wanted to. I think I would have been too frightened of not knowing what to do.

Anyway, I kept my shift on with Michael. The fear was too deep.

Michael got to know Kristin before I did, but if you knew Michael, you had to know me as well, on account of the way we lived. It was one of those instant relationships: she just moved in on our lives; there wasn't any hanging around, no maybes or caution. She knew a whole lot more than we did. She was truly educated—not just stuck in a rut of German Expressionism, which was really all we rated in the ignorance of back-then. She was as glad to find us as we were to find her. She hadn't connected much with anyone in the art school in Dun Laoghaire; she was kind of standoffish, and you had to understand how obsessed she was with her work.

With her work, and with the need to get away from Norway and her family and her upbringing—a need which wasn't exactly unfamiliar to us in Ireland, where it often featured as the overwhelming screw-up in at least half our lives. If it wasn't escape that was your obsession, then likely as not it was the opposite—the longing to belong. Even worse was being caught inside both these states, feeling like some sort of manic pendulum endlessly rushing between the two.

So we just assumed she was the same as the rest of us, that somewhere along the line the claustrophobia had really got to her, and so she'd left. It was a long time before she brought herself to spell out what was really driving her need to escape, and even when she explained, we didn't fully understand what she was trying to tell us.

Michael was an aberration. She didn't want to be in love with him; her body had betrayed her, not her heart. She thought she'd built a wall between the two, but in the end it hadn't worked like that. She couldn't keep them separate; the wall had just dissolved. I don't think Michael knew this. I think he thought that she wanted him in her bed, but only till she stopped wanting him in her bed, and all the time he was waiting for her to wake up one morning and tell him she was moving on. He never said this, only hinted when we were alone together, when we filled the glasses, passed the joint, undressing, but not quite down to bare flesh, still not taking off our shifts.

When Michael moved into Kristin's flat he left me in the studio, alone.

I can't believe I've written that. I can't accept the self-pity.

Nonetheless, I have to admit that was how it felt.

I didn't stay there long. We'd graduated anyway, so there wasn't any need to be over on that side of town. I gave in my notice and rented a room in a shared house in Irishtown, which was walking distance from Michael and Kristin but far enough away from them to give us all the illusion of independence. Then I set about building a life that pretended it didn't revolve around them.

Kristin had this uncle she would sometimes talk about when she was drunk. His name was Otto, and he didn't live in Norway. He was an airline pilot; he didn't really live anywhere; he had a flat in Chicago which he used as a base, but that was all. Kristin seemed to think this was the best way to live. In fact, as we got used to Otto's appearance in her conversation, we began to understand that Otto's escape from Norway seemed to Kristin to be in some way miraculous. She wanted above all else to inherit this gift of not-belonging, to walk in his footsteps and never own anything or love anyone and, above all, never go home. How does it go in the carol? *Heat was in the very sod/that the saint had printed.* Only Uncle Otto was no saint, and his footsteps were full up with ice, not heat—which suited Kristin, who wasn't on the lookout for poor men to feed and warm.

The first time I'd brought Kristin home I'd taken her into the barn at evening and walked her around though the pens, and I knew she was liking the smells and the strangeness of being so close to those big, warm beasts. Some of them pressed up close and snuffled her hands and licked at her clothes, and she stood still and offered her sleeve to their curious tongues. There'd been two young bulls in a pen in the corner, hardly more than babes, well used to being handled. They'd swung their great heads down over the rail and smelled at her clothes.

It was the evening after that visit that she'd told us about the Quisling connection. My mother had just been diagnosed with cancer—something we all knew but didn't speak of. Perhaps it was this that had stirred Kristin's past. The darkness underneath the quiet domestic surface. The secret everyone knew but never referred to.

Michael had opened a bottle of wine; we were in their flat, looking at pictures of Berlin under the Nazis: a book that someone had lent us, the sort of thing you see all the time now, though it wouldn't have had much circulation in the Ireland of the early '90s. Michael was fascinated—the banners, the jackboots, the sieg heils. Kristin was getting quieter. Then she came out with it.

She said her grandmother had been Quisling's youngest sister.

"My mother was his favourite niece. My Uncle Otto was his nephew."

A Quisling. We knew the phrase—it meant a traitor. And yet it took us a moment or two to place the man himself, and in those moments, there must have been a certain blankness in the way we looked back at her.

She stared at us, watching the history lessons we'd half-forgotten click into place.

"Quisling was Norway's chief warmonger," she said helpfully. "He was the man who snuggled up to Hitler. Seized power when the Germans invaded Norway, then ran the country for the fascists till they were defeated."

"Does she mind?" The question was out before I could stop myself. I couldn't believe how inane my own voice sounded.

"Mind being the niece of Norway's Petain?"

She went over to a shelf, lifted down a file and extracted one of those creased, sepia-coloured photographs you can create now on the computer with one click on an icon. (Well, not quite. You can make it go sepia, but the yellowed paper and the crinkled cracks are harder to achieve.)

We stared at the photo. A man in some sort of formal regalia was holding a very young baby in a long white christening dress. Four men wearing SS uniforms were ranged around them. There were champagne flutes in their hands. Kristin said the baby was her mother. As well as being her uncle, Quisling had been her godfather.

"He was executed in 1945. It's the only photo of the christening I've ever seen. She thinks it was burned with the rest."

What could we do with information such as this? It was like being handed a small chunk of something which we hadn't known was live uranium, only when we touched the lump it somehow lost its potency and turned into a curio.

She watched us, our puzzled, ambiguous reactions. Then she started to laugh. It was awful; I'd have felt better if she'd cried.

By now Kristin was getting her work shown, and not just in Ireland. Portraits—always in black and white and always with some quality that stays present to the inner eye. Michael was barely scratching a living, filling in Film Council grant forms, working at anything that came up. Kristin had wangled me a few hours modelling for life classes in the Art College where she worked, and as well as that, I was painting. When I wasn't painting, I was cleaning for a woman who lived in Sandymount and wanted someone who didn't seem like a cleaner and wouldn't disapprove of the way she lived.

Mam had had a course of chemotherapy, and they seemed to think she'd be okay. I went home when I could, but I was working hard. I couldn't afford to hang around; I had to get some work together, or it was the boat to England and an advertising agency, if I was lucky.

On my next visit home, Kristin and Michael came too. The yearling bulls had been distributed in labeled plastic bags in various freezers, but the heifers were alive and breeding. They crowded round and licked and snuffled her just like the last time.

"I think they know we've met before." Kristin held out an arm, offering her hand for inspection.

My sister Sarah was there. She was already following Michael, though she'd never normally have volunteered for the cowshed.

"They remember your smell," Sarah said. "Especially if you're the one that minds them. When we had milking cows it was Mammy who did the milking. Sometimes she'd go to Wexford to visit her mam. Only a couple of days, but when she came home, they'd all stand around her and sniff."

I stared at Sarah. It was true what she'd just said, but it was even less like her to talk about life-on-the-farm than it was for her to pay the cows a visit.

I never saw anyone fall for anyone else the way Sarah fell for Michael. She trailed around after him the whole weekend, she was fairly sick with love. Michael was embarrassed, and Kristin tried to look the other way. She wasn't the only one—we were all doing our level best to pretend we'd gone suddenly blind. Except for Mammy. I was in the garden digging leeks for the table when I heard Mammy's voice from the other side of the wall. She was asking Sarah was she twenty-one or twelve?

Sarah got the bus back to Dublin that Sunday night, but Kristin and Michael and I stayed on at the farm for another two days. Sarah lived in Rathmines in a flat with two girls she'd shared with all through college. I hardly saw her except when our paths crossed at home. She was five years younger than me, and we had nothing in common except for the birth-accident of both having spent our formative years looking out the same windows. She worked in an estate agent's office off Stephen's Green. Jobs weren't easily come by—then as now—so you had to forget about that degree you'd thought was going to change your life and settle for whatever came your way. Unless you wanted to teach or emigrate—they were still options.

Sarah had never felt she belonged on the farm, and her city job was boring and menial. She was clever and ambitious and pretty. She'd had more than enough of accepting what fate threw at her. This time she was going to fight.

Five weeks later, Michael told Kristin that he and Sarah were seeing each other. Then he said that maybe in fairness to both, he should be moving out.

Michael thought he was buying himself time, keeping them both hanging round while he thought things over and made a decision.

Michael was very attractive. He was well used to women competing for him, but this time he hadn't understood how high the stakes were. Kristin was not just the most talented human being I've ever known; the two of them were mentally attuned on a level that's rare enough in any partnership and invaluable to an artist. I'd no idea he'd started seeing Sarah in Dublin, and I still don't know how she wriggled her way so deep into his life. By getting into his bed, that much was obvious—but how did she pull off a wedding? That's what I'll never figure out.

A few days after Michael had moved out, I heard Kristin's voice through my sleep. I woke up and stuck my head out through the open window, and there she was, standing on the pavement, looking up. I threw down the keys and listened to the front door opening and her feet on the stairs. The next thing she was in the room beside me, saying she couldn't seem to fall asleep without another body in the bed, and did I mind if she climbed in beside me? It wasn't really a question. She kicked off her trainers, unzipped her jeans and wriggled out of her sweater. She was awake when she reached for the covers, but I think she was asleep before she hit the sheet. I left her there, still sleeping, in the morning. When I got back that evening, she had gone.

I'd taken the photos at the wedding, and I still have one of Kristin that I keep in a drawer in my desk. The strange thing is that I can't remember taking it. I think when a situation is straining you almost to breaking, you stop being conscious of what you're doing, your being acts by itself.

Michael had insisted on the invitation. He didn't want to lose her, wanted everything to go on being the way it had been: Sarah in his bed, Kristin as his colleague and his friend. Sex with Sarah must have addled Michael's brain because he wasn't normally that insensitive. Sarah kept her mouth shut—she was tough, my sister Sarah. She wasn't going to let one invitation spoil her day.

And Kristin? Something to do with courage, with not backing off, with refusing her mother's acceptance of a shame she'd had no part in creating.

The photo is a back view of Kristin standing at the field gate. It was May—early May—the lilacs just out, the cows sitting down in grass that was suddenly lush and so long that they'd only to stretch their necks out to feed. Their calves, still not weaned, were wandering about. Kristin's hair has pulled loose from its clips, she's taken her sandals off, her feet are hidden by the springing grass.

After the wedding, Kristin applied for a green card. She got it, but it took a long time to come through. The irony was that Michael and Sarah had gone to Australia, but they didn't like it, so they ended up in America as well. No one knew the Celtic Tiger was lurking round the corner, just getting ready to roar.

Mammy's dead now. She died two weeks before Kristin left for the U.S. The back end of January, the time she thought best for dying.

She'd had six children, and she'd read *Gone with the Wind* in the final stages of each pregnancy. Aside from that, she read very little except for *The Farmer's Journal.* I don't know why she "took leave of her senses" (her own words) and immersed herself in Scarlett O'Hara's melodramas before each delivery. I have her copy still, and I've never read it, though I've seen the film.

Mammy died when the liver cancer came back. She didn't want any more treatment, so her end was less protracted than it might have been. Sarah sent her a large-print copy of *Gone with the Wind* with a note in it saying she thought it might be easier for her to read. Mammy glanced at it but didn't open it. Sarah hadn't understood that for Mammy it was connected with new lives pushing into the world, not old ones trying to get free of it. Sarah came home for her funeral, but Michael didn't. We were civil enough to each other but were careful not to be left alone in the same room. I found I hated Sarah, and my hatred took me by surprise. I don't know how she felt, but I think we were both afraid of what we might say.

Kristin came down from Dublin for the funeral. She was beside me when we followed the coffin down the aisle, and her arm was round my shoulder at the grave. I don't imagine it was easy, but it never crossed my mind to doubt she'd come.

After Mammy died, I didn't miss her, I was just glad she wasn't dying anymore. But I miss her now, and I wish she was still in the kitchen, stirring something or folding washing or wiping the eggs she brought in from the hens. I can't stand people who go on about the kitchen tasks their mothers did when they were children. It's as though that was all their mothers were—the ones who made bread or hung out the washing or made the jam. As though they only existed because of their place in the child's experience.

But underneath, I'm not so harsh. I know they're really saying this woman's life was the life of the house, and of everyone in it.

So I want her to be here still, stirring or folding or cleaning eggs, because then I feel safe. I don't like myself for wanting to have her back so I can feel this way. I know that safety is a fiction we cling to as children and then spend our lives growing up from. But I'm one of those people who'll always think "mother" and "warm" go together. I understand there are those who don't make this connection.

When someone close to you dies, what happens on the outside is so immediate that you hardly realise the enormity of the internal movement that has taken place. When half the hillside has fallen away, you see through to valleys and mountains its contours have concealed.

At first there's only naked stone beneath the landslide; then gradually small mosses and ferns take root, and pockets of soil accumulate. With more time, young trees will spring from these pocks, and the harsh grey slope will be wooded. The years pass. You forget these new contours and ridges were once other than they are now.

Nothing can stop this process if there is time and support, but if more landslides come too hard on the first, those small beginnings of growth will be swept away. The rock slope stays bare.

That was how it was for me, anyway. Mammy died, then Kristin left, then Tommy turned over the tractor on Neil. Ordinary things that happen to anyone. Not wars or famines or camps, but enough.

When his health began to make his profession impractical, Uncle Otto had left the airline and taken a job as an instructor at a local airfield. He never went home, not even to bury his parents. Sometimes Kristin's mother remembered her younger brother's birthday, and sometimes he was in when she phoned. She never made contact at Christmas. She knew too well the pain of those Christmas celebrations in their childhood.

Uncle Otto had been diagnosed with lung cancer in its early stages, but he told no one. He didn't give up drinking or smoking, he didn't want treatment, he died in an all-night drinking place—a coughing fit, then his heart stopped. Kristin phoned me to tell me. She said she was under pressure from her parents. They'd called from Norway and asked her to go there, make sure all the documents were in the right envelopes, formalities completed, nothing left lying around to follow them into the future.

"What do you think I should do?"

She'd never asked my opinion before; she just said what she was going to do and did it. I was so surprised that I answered without any thought of what I was saying.

"Forget him. That's what he wanted. Let him alone."

She went anyway. She phoned me from his flat. She said there were no letters, no photos, no cell phone, just four numbers scribbled onto the wall above the land line. She'd rung them all, but the first two had been disconnected. The third was a cell phone, a woman who said her name was Linda. Linda said she'd stopped knowing Otto because she smoked herself and she didn't want to watch herself encouraging him to die. She said she'd been quite straight about this with Otto because he was the sort of man you could be straight with. She said she'd missed him, but he couldn't change and neither could she.

The fourth number turned out to be his doctor's.

I still saw Sarah at family gatherings; her four American children were brought "home" one by one and introduced. Somehow Michael always contrived things to ensure he was not there at the same time I was. Perhaps it was better this way. What would I have said to Michael? How could I have borne his presence if I'd had to look him in the eye? All my life I had stood beside sinks drying dishes with Sarah, slicing cakes, filling sandwiches, setting out glasses, teapots, cups. We were used to functioning together on this physical level, though the tasks we performed were so intimate that it was harder to bear the hostility between us. At least we could work without talking.

When I'd closed the door on Sarah, I'd thought that somehow I could shut down some of the pain of what I'd always feel for Kristin. But real life is never this stark or uncluttered; it's unruly, disordered and as full of emotional snarl-ups as the fine garden netting I struggle to keep in place round the vegetable patch. The birds make holes and pass in and out, the wind tears streamers of net from the uprights, they blow and tangle and knot. I repair the damage as best I can, but there's always more wind, more birds.

The message that Sarah left on my phone was all about Michael and Kristin. Sarah was clearly beside herself. Among the rage and hysteria, I worked out that Michael had left her for Kristin. Sarah thought I knew all about it.

Today is the last day of the rest of my life and the first day of the rest of my life. This is true every day. There are no divisions, though sometimes there are external changes that seem like divisions.

Everything happens both inside and outside, but sometimes what happens on the outside is so painful that you try to stop it from gaining access to the place inside you, where you live. This can be done for a while, but ultimately nothing can stop the slow seep-through.

Then again, sometimes it all happens on the inside, and there's hardly an external mark to be seen.

Like today. Today is hazy, though the sun is trying to burn off the cloud. The cerise tulips under the pear tree are starting to die.

The lilac has formed dark purple cones of flowers which haven't yet opened.

A book arrives, your sister phones. Small events in themselves.

The emotions inside me now come from huge things that happened on the outside years ago. They're here now because they've finally made it all the way through.

I wheel the overfull barrow down to a dumping place and tip.

I wish Kristin had told me when she came here for that photograph last spring; I wish she'd trusted me that much. But then perhaps she hadn't started seeing him again.

Or perhaps she'd never stopped.

I wish I'd told Kristin how much I was in love with her those years ago. I wish I'd trusted her that much.

But then again, perhaps I've never stopped.

I wheel the barrow back up. I sort through the tubers I've saved and do a final inspection to check for the white, thready roots of the common vetch. The scutch grass is easier. Its big, brutal underground shoots come out in one piece if the ground's halfway dry. Vetch roots break off, and the next thing you know there's a batch of new shoots pushing up. A bit like despair, a state of mind which has a habit of reappearing when you think it's cleared.

Banned

Laura Venita Green

Lainey's weekend bag sat by the garage door, and a pot of coffee was nearly finished brewing when a text came through from her sister: *DON'T!!!* She'd been ready to say goodbye to her husband, Kevin, and her stepdaughter, Mena, and to start the five-hour drive from Austin to west Louisiana for her dad's seventy-fifth birthday. She hadn't been back home since she'd left for a job more than two decades ago. When she left, her little sister had banned her from returning to their home. Over the years, she'd extended that ban to include their town, their parish, the entire state.

Guess you told Amelia, she texted to her dad's phone, and the dot-dot-dot danced around for a minute until *Couldn't risk her having an episode when you drove up unannounced. Don't try to get out of coming!* popped up.

She turned off her ringer and put her phone screen down on the kitchen counter, and then she poured herself a cup of coffee. Spilled drops hissed on the burner. Through the window above the sink, she watched the sun rise over Lake Austin. Leading up to the trip, she'd had a ton of nightmares, picked fights with Kevin, overlooked work meetings that she'd requested and marked on her calendar. She took a swig of coffee and gagged a little when she swallowed; she'd forgotten to add milk.

Mena, who hadn't yet gone to bed, entered the kitchen and hung back in the doorway. Three weeks ago, she'd dropped out of her second year of law school and had come to stay with them for an unspecified period of time, quickly adopting a nocturnal life. She held Lainey's miniature schnauzer in the crook of her arm.

"Pepper says *auf Wiedersehen*," Mena said, moving the little dog's paw up and down in a gentle wave. The other dog, a mastiff mix, lumbered in at the sound of her voice. "Shadow just says *auf, auf*."

Lainey tried to smile. She bent over and leaned her forehead on the countertop.

After a moment she felt Shadow nudge her hip with his nose and heard Mena say, "You're really disappointed in me, aren't you?"

Lainey turned her head and squinted across the room at her stepdaughter, experiencing the sort of disconnect that she sometimes felt as a stepmom. Disappointed? Mena was a twenty-eight-year-old grown woman. She'd already been fifteen when Lainey had started dating her dad, eighteen when they'd married. She'd gone away to college, graduated with a studio arts degree, and moved to Brooklyn, lived with a bunch of roommates, paid her rent bartending, and created incredibly intricate large-scale textile art mostly from found objects. A few years ago, several Brooklyn-based artists had broken into the padlocked old Domino Sugar Refinery in Williamsburg for an unsanctioned art exhibition. Lainey and Kevin had ducked under a fence and climbed through a broken window to attend. One of Mena's tapestries, a night sky packed full of lace stars, covered an entire two-story brick wall of the refinery. She'd spent eighteen months working on it, and it was by far the most dazzling piece in the show. At the end of the night, she had set it on fire. The entire room watched it blaze, and Lainey had stood clutching tightly to Kevin's hand, silently crying in the dark room. The last time she had felt that moved by art had been listening to her sister play the piano when they were girls. Such a long time ago. All this to say that no, Lainey wasn't disappointed. Maybe a little judgey, because it was obvious to anyone that Mena should have never gone to law school—she was an artist—but judgey was different than disappointed. Lainey loved Mena very much, but from a polite distance because they were only thirteen years apart in age, and Mena already had a perfectly functioning mother.

"I think what's happening is that I'm having my first real nervous breakdown."

Mena put the little dog on the countertop, and its nails clicked as it scampered over to Lainey. "Oh. You want to tell me about it?"

Lainey stood and picked up Pepper, putting a hand on Shadow's neck so he didn't feel left out. "It's just my dysfunctional family. My dad wants me to visit for his birthday, but my sister's mentally ill"—Lainey almost never said that aloud, but it was the unavoidable truth—"and she really doesn't want me to come. I don't know. I feel like I have to go, but maybe not."

"Well," Mena said, "I don't have a heck of a lot going on right now, if you think having company would help."

It wasn't that Mena was stuck up or that Lainey was embarrassed by her family. It was just that Mena had grown up with professional parents in a world of education and culture and vacations, and Lainey could picture her forced neutral expression when they drove together onto the dirt road and past the trailer park to get to the house where Lainey grew up. Lainey imagined

Amelia peering at them, paranoid, from behind a curtain while they parked, and then hiding away for the whole visit. Lainey stopped herself from saying "Don't worry about it" and instead said, "Yeah, I'd love company." She saw a light enter Mena's eyes that had been missing lately.

While Mena went to pack a bag, Lainey crawled into bed with Kevin. He wound his body, warm from sleep, around her, and immediately relaxed in his arms.

He slid his hand down her inner thigh and kissed her neck. "Why don't you just Bartleby this trip and stay in bed with me?" he whispered in her ear.

She laughed, and he squeezed her tighter.

"Oh, god, I want to. But I promised my dad and . . . Mena's coming with me now."

At that, Kevin sat up and Lainey rolled onto her back.

"Really?" he said. "How did that happen?"

"Well, she's been up all night, and I asked her to come. I think she could stand to get out of the house, don't you?"

Kevin got up and grabbed his robe from a hook just inside the bathroom door. "Hell, yes, I do," he said. "This is excellent. Try to find out what's going on with her, okay? But no pressure. You know what? Never mind. Just have a great time."

He opened the bedroom door to both dogs, waiting on the other side. He gave them each a vigorous pet and then motioned for Lainey to come on, come on.

Mena sat in the chair by the garage door, ready to go. She wore a strappy summer dress that showed off all the tattoos one of her old Brooklyn roommates had given her. She tensed up a little when Kevin came in grinning, overenthusiastic, holding the dogs back that were already vying to get in on the car ride. She endured a quick hug. Poor guy. His level of parental worry whenever his daughter went through a rough patch was something Lainey understood but could never match in feeling. It was obvious to

Lainey that Mena would stop being so standoffish if he could just be cool. But Kevin had never been good at hiding his true feelings, one of the many things that Lainey loved about him.

He waved goodbye while Lainey backed out of the driveway. Mena reclined the passenger seat and fell asleep before they were even out of the neighborhood.

They got onto Highway 71 and had about eighty miles before they hit I-10 in Columbus, which would take them almost the rest of the way. Lainey drove it in silence, both hands on the steering wheel, breathing in through her nose, out through her mouth. She couldn't shake the feeling that something terrible would happen if she visited home, a feeling that had stopped her from going all the other times she'd tried over the years. Her sister's bans were powerful—Amelia hadn't been able to function without them while they were growing up, so the family had always treated them as reality. But this time her dad had insisted—so unlike him—said he had some news he'd only share in person. Which of course made her think he was dying, and then what would happen to her sister?

Her vision narrowed to a tunnel. She picked out a station wagon driving just under the speed limit and followed it closely all the way to Columbus, where she stopped at a gas station before they got on the interstate. She woke Mena up to use the restroom. As she filled up the tank, she looked at all the texts that had come through from her sister—*Don't come, don't even try. Don't. Don't. Don't!*—and decided that this trip was a no-go; she'd just have to call her dad and tell him it was impossible.

But when Mena came out of the convenience store, she was loaded up with supplies—Snickers, Doritos, Nerds, two Smartwaters, Ziploc bags, a pad of paper, and a pen—and had the giddy manner of a little girl who was getting away with something. She put the waters in their cup holders, threw the junk food in the back seat, and put the Ziplocs, pen, and paper in her lap. She pulled something from the pocket of her dress.

"Look at this," she said. She uncrumpled a piece of cloth and smoothed it out on the dashboard. It was a patch, ragged and dingy gray, with "Gigi" stitched in red. "I saw this hanging off the cashier's shirt. By one single thread. I hadn't even thought about starting another project, but I haven't done any work in forever and I think it's killing me. So I just asked her, can I have that? She looked at me like I was insane, but then she snapped it off and handed it over, just like that."

Mena flipped open the cover on her pad of paper and wrote: *8:43 a.m., April 17, Star Stop 71 gas station.*

"What city are we in?"

"Columbus."

Columbus, TX. With Lainey on road trip to La. Saw this hanging off cashier's shirt by one single thread. She handed it over on request without speaking.

Mena held the Gigi patch to a tattoo-less spot on her upper arm. "Might be good enough to make the collection," she said, then zipped the nametag and the paper into the baggie and beamed up at Lainey. "All good?"

Lainey showed Mena some teeth, the best she could do.

Mena reclined again and shut her eyes. Lainey pulled away from the gas station, feeling nauseous, feeling like she could barely manage a breath, her head hurting so badly she had to squint to get on the interstate. But once she pulled onto the entrance ramp and got moving on I-10, the strangest thing happened—her body relaxed, her senses sharpened, she felt great. Night and day. Maybe it was Mena's enthusiasm, this rare gift of one-on-one bonding, or the idea of seeing her family again after so many years or even believing once and for all that her sister banning her from visiting home wasn't some unbreakable spell. It wasn't.

She put on some music and settled in for the long ride ahead.

Two and a half hours farther down I-10, Lainey found a local NPR station that was re-airing a segment with Yusuf Islam, the artist formerly known as Cat Stevens. They were interviewing him and playing some of the music from his new album.

Mena stirred beside her and sat up, brushing her hair back out of her face. "I need to pee again soon."

Lainey turned the volume down a little bit. "I'll look for the next exit. We could get an early lunch, too, before we cross into Louisiana. This is Cat Stevens. Do you know his stuff?"

Mena didn't answer. She was staring out her window and then turned around in her seat to peer out the back.

"'Peace Train?' 'Moonshadow?' Literally anything on the *Harold and Maude* soundtrack?"

"Lainey?"

Something in Mena's voice made Lainey's heart pound. She tried to ignore it. "My sister used to sing Cat Stevens all the time," she said. "Our mom was such a megafan. Our whole family loved him."

"Lainey? That sign just said Kerrville. Did you not notice that we're in the hill country? That the sun's at our back? That we're going the wrong way down I-10?"

Lainey's fingers began to tingle. She leaned forward in her seat and turned the volume up to maximum, and Mena covered her ears and the interviewer said, "*Do you think you may have benefitted by taking a few years off from the industry*?" and Cat Stevens answered, "*Absolutely, I don't drink, I don't*"—and Mena switched off the radio and Lainey took the exit and pulled to the shoulder of the access road and put the car in park.

Midafternoon, they pulled back into their neighborhood in Austin. They had driven a four-hundred-mile triangle. Lainey knew Kevin was working from home, since he had the house to himself, and walking in there right now and trying to explain herself was too much. She really didn't know what to say.

She paused a couple houses before theirs. She and Mena had both been quiet on the drive back, even when they'd stopped for lunch, but now she said, "You know I love your dad very much, right?"

Mena turned to look at her. "You don't want to go home right now, do you?"

Lainey shook her head.

"I get it. My dad's the type of person who has never turned the wrong way on the highway."

No, Lainey wanted to say. No, that's not the reason. But it was close enough to the reason, and she didn't have the energy to lie about it.

They checked into a place on Lake Austin, just a few miles from their house, some rental cabins owned by Mena's high school friend, Sam. The day had turned hot, and Lainey was out on their screened-in porch with the door open so she could feel the breeze from the river.

Earlier, on the walk from reception to their cabin, Lainey had seen a few miniature horses grazing around the property. Now one of them clomped its hooves up the two wooden steps to her porch. As if it were right at home, it hopped up onto the deep porch swing, not seeming to mind that it rocked wildly, and curled into Lainey's side, bumping her with its head until she stroked its mane. It had some caked-on dirt in its fur and smelled of hay and manure, but Lainey didn't mind. Because of her sister's aversion to animals, she hadn't been able to have pets while they were growing up, but Lainey loved them. Careful not to break contact with the horse for too long, she texted Kevin a double pink heart emoji to his *Don't forget to have fun!* Then she texted her dad to say that she wouldn't be there today after all. Right away, he called, but she declined it, so he texted back, *Don't let Amelia get to you. I need you to come and you know I don't ask a lot.*

Mena and Sam came in with a bunch of shopping bags. Lainey had met Sam once or twice before, years ago, when he and Mena had acted together in their high school plays, when he'd been an awkward bucktoothed teenager. Now he was a surprisingly tall bucktoothed man.

He saw the miniature horse. "Connie, you know better than that."

Connie kicked her legs out, neighed, and burrowed her head in Lainey's armpit. The swing jerked beneath them.

"No. *Connie*! No," Sam said.

Lainey hugged her entire body around the horse and then pressed her softly away. "You'd better listen, Connie. I'll see you later, girl. Don't worry."

The horse huffed out a breath, and a shower of snot sprayed Lainey's chest and chin. Departing, she snapped her teeth at Sam and looked back at Lainey with big, longing eyes.

"We're taking complete care of you," Mena said. "We're stocked up, and I'm cooking you a gourmet dinner."

Lainey hadn't known that Mena cooked, and she made a mental note to stop treating her like such a guest when she was staying with them.

Mena rifled through one of the shopping bags and found a pair of cuticle scissors that she tore from the package. Then inspected the inside porch screen until she found an excess piece hanging loose from where it was connected to the window frame. She cut off a little section and logged it in and put it in a Ziploc. Sam took a sprig of wildflowers from a vase on the side table and handed it to Mena. She logged that in, too.

After dinner, Mena sat with Lainey on the swing, and they shared a six-pack of Lone Star. The sun had gone down, and a fat June bug circled the light and occasionally heaved its body against the screen, causing Mena to flinch each time.

Mena opened her second bottle of beer and put the cap in one of the plastic baggies she had in her pocket. "I'll log that in later," she said. "You want to tell me what's going on?"

"I feel like I'm the one who should be asking you," Lainey said.

Mena groaned. "Please, don't. Really, the reason I'm staying with you guys and not my mom is that she starts crying every time she sees me and says, 'What's wrong? What's wrong with my baby!?' At least with my dad, I know he'll wait for me to talk. I just have to endure his looks."

Mena plucked one of Connie's mane hairs from Lainey's shirt, rolled it around her finger, and then stuffed the loop into a baggie. Lainey leaned down to get another beer.

"If you don't want to talk to me about it, I'm good with that," Mena said. "I have to say, though, I'm not sure I even knew that you had a sister, which is slightly disturbing. I mean, I met your dad briefly at your wedding, and I know your mom died when you were young, but how did I not know that?"

Lainey thought back to last Thanksgiving when they all—she and Kevin, Mena, Mena's mom, and her husband—had dinner together, as they did occasionally. She could picture herself sitting erect, hands folded neatly on the table, attentive and pleasant the whole time. Chitchatting but never offering anything real. Polite. If she was honest with herself, she acted this way any time Mena was around, receding so as not to detract from father-daughter time. From time with *real* family.

"Hold this. I need to show you something," Lainey said and handed Mena her beer. She went in the cabin to her suitcase and unzipped the inside pocket, pulled out the letter from her sister that she'd kept all these years, that she'd located in a storage box after her dad had told her to come for his birthday.

She climbed back onto the swing and handed the envelope to Mena. Then she shined her phone flashlight on the letter so Mena could see in the dim room. Mena pulled the letter out of the envelope, and a couple paper cutouts of musical notes fell from the envelope onto her lap. The June bug darted from the overhead light and zoomed between their heads, plunking into the screen behind them.

"Jesus!" Mena said. "Ugh!"

The beetle circled back and went for the flashlight, divebombing the illuminated letter. Mena yelled out and slapped at her lap, but before she could crush it, Lainey cupped the June bug in her palms, walked it outside, and released it gently into the night.

"Okay, now we can read it in peace." Even though she'd located the letter, Lainey had been unable to reread it. But she found she could read it alongside Mena.

Amelia's long, slanted print brought Lainey back to the last time she'd really insisted on going to visit. She and Kevin were engaged and had just returned from an entire month in Italy. By that point she hadn't seen her sister in almost ten years, and enough was enough. She'd go and make Amelia accept her back into her life, convince her to attend the wedding. But then this letter arrived by FedEx the day before the visit. Lainey had read it through once, immediately stored it away, and canceled her trip. She hadn't tried to go back since.

Hi Lainey,
DON'T forget you're the love of my life. EVER look deep within yourself and question your soul? COME to terms, as I have, that sacrifices must be made. BACK then it was just the two of us against everyone else. TO the future, though, is where we should look. LOUISIANA, you made clear, is not the place for you. YOU hath awakened from the dream of life, Lainey! ARE you remembering when we saw that etched into the cross? BANNED forever from this world so that you might thrive in the next.
xoxo forever,
Amelia

Mena read out the highlighted words: "Don't. Ever. Come. Back. To. Louisiana. You. Are. Banned." Then she turned over the letter and looked at the back, where Amelia had cut out little paper musical notes and pasted them onto a hand-drawn staff.

"It's part of Beethoven's 'Für Elise.' Amelia's a wonderful musician."

Mena folded up the letter and put it in the envelope. She gathered the loose musical notes and was about to drop them in the envelope, but Lainey said, "You can keep one if you want," and Mena picked out a delicate sixteenth note and placed it carefully in a baggie.

"One last beer while you tell me more about her?" Mena said, and Lainey stretched out her hand to receive the offering.

A little more than an hour into their trip the next morning—this time with Mena in the driver's seat—and they were passing that same gas station in Columbus.

"Thanks again, Gigi!" Mena said, waving to the convenience store, and then she entered I-10 going in the correct direction.

Lainey leaned her seat back, stared out the sunroof, and tried to calm her racing heart. Mena had downloaded all the episodes of a popular podcast called *Hellseer,* about a psychic in New Orleans named Madame Trinae. The podcast was produced by the psychic's daughter, Abby Richard. Abby was open about her lifelong struggles with addiction, and she had used the podcast's wild success to start a Kickstarter campaign for opioid-addiction treatment centers and Narcan distribution, which had raised over two million dollars. Lainey had meant to listen to it—it was what everyone at work and all her friends were talking about—but she hadn't gotten around to it. And three episodes in, passing Beaumont, she'd barely paid any attention.

"I don't think I can do this," she said, but she'd whispered it, and the radio volume was too loud for Mena to hear.

In no time, they were bypassing Orange, and Lainey began to drip with sweat. She closed the windows and maxed out the AC. She could now see the bridge that spanned the Sabine, the river that marked the border between Texas and Louisiana. On the podcast, Madame Trinae, who was hosting a group of skeptical scientists from MIT, suddenly spoke in a voice that seemed directed at Lainey, cutting through her haze: *I'm from the west part of the state, originally from a place called Rosepine. Very rural, very insular. And I found, once I left, It wasn't possible to go back. Now if you think about—* Lainey clicked the radio off, and the sudden lack of sound packed the car, making the space claustrophobic.

They passed the Texas Visitor Center on the left. Just up ahead, seconds away, was the final Texas exit that looped back around to the Visitor Center. Lainey yelled, "Pull over!" and Mena said, "What? I can't," and Lainey said, "PULL OVER PULL OVER PULL OVER," and lunged for the steering wheel.

Mena pulled off at the last possible second, and the car fishtailed but straightened out. They took the U-turn to the left under the interstate, and as soon as they were going west again, Lainey could breathe. And then they were parked at the Visitor Center.

Their Airbnb landlady, Bertie, charged sixty-five dollars for the two spare rooms in her house and another eighteen each if they opted for dinner, which Mena had when she'd set it all up from the Visitor Center. They were now in a rural Texas town about twenty miles from the Louisiana border and about forty miles from where Lainey's dad and sister lived. Mena had taken over everything. While Lainey paced around the Visitor Center, Mena had even spoken to Lainey's dad and explained that they wouldn't be there today for his birthday after all. Then she'd texted Kevin that all was well but that they were officially "off the grid" and they'd see him Sunday.

As soon as they checked in, Lainey locked herself in her bedroom, curled up under the homemade quilt, and slept. At six-thirty, she went down to dinner as scheduled. The dining room table was set for three, and Mena was already seated when Lainey walked in.

"Look," Mena said, pressing her lips together in amusement and stretching her arms out wide to showcase one of the walls in the wood-paneled dining room. The entire wall was covered in red, white, and blue tassels that hung from hooks in the pattern of an American flag. Small tassels for the stars, large for the stripes. "If you were wondering why we're staying in this lady's house instead of some hotel, this is it. There were at least a dozen pictures of this one wall on the website, and I couldn't pass it up. I am not leaving here without a tassel."

Lainey smiled. "You're in a good mood."

"I've been working and making big plans all day. Plus, how can one not be in a good mood in the presence of this stunning work of genius?"

Lainey sat across from Mena and left the space at the head of the table open.

Through the double swinging doors that led to the kitchen, the landlady, Bertie, entered with a bubbling hot dish. "King Ranch casserole," she said, and set it on a potholder in the center of the table. The woman was elderly and very small, and her hands shook with the heavy dish, but she dismissed their attempts at helping. Then she made some other rounds and came in with green beans and bacon, mashed sweet potatoes, and a simple green salad.

She sat down with them, and they passed the food around.

Lainey took her first bite of casserole and had to cover her mouth with her hand and breathe out some of the heat. It was delicious. Mena was also finishing her first bite. "Oh, wow. This is great," she said.

Bertie nodded. "Do you want some wine?"

"Yes, please," Lainey said. She wasn't in the mood to interact with a stranger, but wine would definitely help.

"Me too," Mena said.

Bertie struggled up from her chair and went back into the kitchen. She came back with a box of wine in one hand and three plastic juice cups on a tray. The cups were large, and she filled them each to the brim.

Lainey smiled politely and took a sip. It was bad enough—vinegary and bitter—that she winced a little, but she knew from experience that the next sip wouldn't be half as bad, and with enough perseverance it would even start to taste good.

Through the first half of the excellent dinner and bad wine, no one said much. But then Bertie broke the silence. "So, you two are friends? How do you know each other?"

Before Lainey could answer, Mena said, "Yeah, sure. You could say we're friends."

Bertie looked at them sideways. "Are you one of those same-sex couples?"

"What?" Mena said. "No."

"Don't think I mind it," Bertie said. "I may be ninety-two, but I'm not living in the dark ages."

"Ninety-two, Bertie?" Mena said. "I swear you don't look a day past eighty-nine. And come on, we rented both rooms."

"Yes, but that's what you would do, isn't it? If you didn't want me—"

"I'm married to her dad," Lainey said before Bertie could finish.

At this, Bertie's face darkened. "But you two are the same age."

"Not quite." Lainey said.

"Ah, well. Tale as old as time." Bertie sighed and then downed half of her wine.

After dinner, Bertie invited them to play a game over dessert, and Mena said, "Yes, definitely!" at the same time Lainey said "No, I don't think so." Bertie accepted the answer she preferred, cleared the table, and brought in a Tupperware container with hundreds of tiny puzzle pieces.

"You two spread these out. I'm going to go get Pete."

Lainey spilled the pieces onto the table. Several fell to the carpet, and when she bent over to pick them up, she felt a little lightheaded. "I guess we're doing a jigsaw with Bertie. And . . . Pete? A typical Friday night."

"Um, yeah. This night is an actual dream come true for me, it's so insane." Mena was acting more like her old self—funny, extroverted, interested in the world around her—a self that Lainey hadn't seen in quite some time. Mena got up and went over to the wall of tassels. She took a red one off its hook and turned it upside down. "Damn it," she said. "I was planning on snipping a piece from the inside where no one would notice, but they're hand braided. Way too delicate. The whole thing would unravel."

"Put that back," Bertie said, walking in with a bird cage covered by a towel. She put the cage in the middle of the table and uncovered it. Inside danced a green and yellow parakeet. "Pete likes to hang out after dinner."

"Hi, sweet bird," Lainey said.

Pete hopped to the side of his cage where Lainey sat and began to bob his head up and down, watching her.

"Can I have one of these?" Mena said, still holding the tassel.

"No, you may not," Bertie said.

"Oh, come on! These are amazing."

Pete rattled his cage at Lainey and sang and then in an oddly robotic voice, said, "*Watabu tuglibir.*"

"I know they're amazing. I made them. I hand dye them, too, so if you take one, I'm not going to be able to make another that exactly matches."

Lainey leaned toward the cage, and Pete jumped up and down. "*Watabu tuglibir.*"

Mena put back the red tassel and picked up a white. "Then give me one of these. They're not dyed."

Bertie was almost a foot shorter than Mena but had no problem grabbing the tassel out of her hand. "I treat the white ones so they don't yellow. You may not have one, pushy girl."

They took their seats, and Bertie topped off their cups and then scooted a crystal dish filled with hard candies from the opposite end of the table. Dessert.

Now Pete was really going wild, flapping his wings and clawing at the shredded paper towel at the bottom of his cage. "*Watabu tuglibir. Watabu tublibir. Watabu tuglibir.*"

"Oh, you have a new girlfriend, do you?" Bertie said to Pete in a babyish voice. "What a butt-ugly bird. Yes, you are. Yes, you are." She turned to Lainey and said, "Mind if I let him out?"

"Not at all."

Bertie opened the cage, and immediately Pete flew and perched on the top of Lainey's head. Lainey put her hand up with one finger out and held it to the bird. He hopped on, and she transferred him to her shoulder. He walked sideways and cuddled his body into her neck and calmed down. The soft feathers on her neck felt nice. So did the wine.

"Any friend of Pete is a friend of mine," Bertie said. "I've completely changed my mind about you."

Mena snorted and spilled wine down the front of her dress, and Bertie grinned at her and then found a corner puzzle piece and positioned it at the corner of the table.

"Are you in school, young lady?" Bertie asked.

"Well, I'm twenty-eight," Mena said and after a pause added, "But I was in law school until about three weeks ago."

"And?" Bertie said. "Even I know law school doesn't let out in April."

"And now I'm not. I got kicked out."

Lainey had been feeling pleasantly removed from everything, falling into her comfort zone of fading into the background, but this got her attention. "No, you didn't. You quit."

"No, I didn't. I got kicked out."

"Oh, boy," Bertie said.

Then Mena told them how she had plagiarized a paper, but since her dad was an Alum of the Year and a very important person, they asked if she'd like to quit, wink, wink. She told them how she'd been plagiarizing all semester and they'd pretended not to notice until she made it so blatant that it was impossible for them to look the other way.

"Oh, Mena," Lainey said.

Mena suddenly seemed annoyed. "Are you disappointed now?"

"'Disappointed' assumes that I have some sort of greater wisdom. I don't."

"Well, I'm disappointed," Bertie said. "That all just sounds stupid."

"Thank you!" Mena said.

"Do you want me to be disappointed?" Lainey said. "I mean, I'm definitely feeling a little like 'WTF, fellow human,' but that's different."

Mena said, "If WTF is what I can get from you, I'll take it."

Everyone was quiet for a moment. Lainey couldn't figure out why Mena seemed angry with her all of a sudden. She put a cinnamon candy in her mouth and let it dissolve in her cheek. It burned a little.

"Sounds to me like it's time to embrace our disappointment," Bertie said. She raised her plastic cup, tapped her watch band, and Pete flew up to it and held on. Mena raised her cup too, and so did Lainey.

Bertie said, "To disappointment."

"To disappointment," Lainey said.

"Here, here," Mena said.

They drank, and Bertie refilled their cups and started sifting through the puzzle pieces again. "Okay, let's get down to business. And you," she said, pointing a finger in Mena's face. "Don't cheat."

Mena threw her hands up. "Come on! You can't cheat at a jigsaw puzzle!"

"You'd find a way, I have no doubt," Bertie said. "I've got my eye on you."

"*Watabu tuglibir,*" Pete said when he perched back on Lainey's shoulder.

The next morning, head splitting from cheap wine and mouth cottony from dehydration, Lainey was ready to go home a day earlier than planned. Ready to lie in bed and cry to Kevin and let him take care of her. But after breakfast, when Lainey brought her bag out to the car, Mena was loading the trunk with a cooler and camping supplies that she'd carried from Bertie's garage.

"What are you doing?" Lainey said. "It's time to give up, Mena."

"Too bad. I've made plans. Don't worry, we're not entering Louisiana, but we're getting very close."

Bertie came out, wearing a floral muumuu and slippers. Her white, wispy hair brushed her collarbone. She pulled Lainey down to her height and kissed her cheek; then she called to Mena, "I want everything intact when you bring it back. Don't snap a pole or go jabbing a bunch of holes in the tent canvas."

"Oh, my god," Mena said and got in the driver's seat.

They both waved to Bertie, and Lainey asked if this meant they had to come back by and drop everything off later. She was exhausted.

"Don't worry. I booked three nights next month for a tassel lesson. She said she can manage to not go camping until then."

Within half an hour they were parked in the nearly empty lot of a Baptist church that was situated next to some woods. When they got out of the car, Lainey could hear organ music through the walls, someone practicing inside. They didn't have cell service here, but Mena was able to pull up the GPS on her phone, and Lainey could see that their blinking blue dot wasn't far off from a red pin next to the Sabine River.

"There should be a trail over there," Mena said, pointing to a shed at the corner of the lot. They got their bags and equipment and set out.

Lainey followed, going along, enduring whatever Mena had planned for one last day. She trudged through the brush and slipped on some moss when she tried to climb over a log that had fallen in their path. She picked herself up and kept going.

After a little while, she could hear the rush of the river ahead of them. And then she could see it, wide, the water clear and rushing over large, flat rocks. Shallow enough to walk across. And there it was—Louisiana—right in front of them, woods, dirt, shore, all exactly the same as on their side.

At the water, Mena looked around and rechecked the GPS. She seemed lost. There really wasn't any place to camp, no clearing to set up a tent, Lainey saw. Maybe that meant they could give up this odyssey and go home. But then Mena yelled out, "Hello?! Can you hear me?" and right away a voice in the distance called back to them.

"Is that . . . ?" Lainey said.

They went in the direction of the voice. They had to skirt the shore around a bend and push through a thick tangle of shrubs, but then they were at a clearing, and sure enough, he was there, across the shore. Lainey's dad. Too far away to see completely clearly, but still, she'd known the pitch of his voice, and she recognized the way he stood with his hips jutting slightly forward in his green plaid shirt and jeans. The trees were thicker on his side. No clearing to camp. He was alone.

"He looks healthy," Mena said. "He looks better than when I saw him ten years ago."

He did. He looked bigger, stronger, not the same stooped, defeated man who had showed up briefly at her wedding, eroding a little of the joy she'd felt on that day.

Her dad called out to them, but the river drowned out his voice. She and Mena cupped their hands to their ears.

He mimed pitching a baseball, and Mena jumped up and yelled, "Yes!"

He threw something underhand, and it dropped in the water close to their shore. Mena picked it up before the river could carry it off. She handed it to Lainey. Wrapped in a trash bag and then a dishtowel was an old walkie-talkie, just like she and Amelia had had when they were little.

Lainey turned it on, and it crackled, and then, "Well, hey, kiddo. Over."

Lainey sat cross-legged on the sand, and Mena sat beside her.

"Hey, Dad. Over"

On the other shore, he was gesturing toward the trees, saying something, and then a woman walked out from behind a thick trunk. She was tall, overweight, dressed in a black T-shirt and khaki shorts. Her thick white legs were so pasty that they almost had an inner glow against the brown-gray-green of the shore and tree trunks. How often did she get out of the house? Her blond hair was long, stringy, and she kept it in her face, almost completely hiding her eyes as she shuffled over toward their father.

Lainey's chest felt so tight she thought she might suffocate. She heard a soft cry escape her and then Mena's hand was in hers, squeezing tight.

The woman across the river, her sister, Amelia, would be thirty-seven now. When Lainey had left home, Amelia was only fifteen. Lainey had practically raised her and then never saw her again. Not even a picture because her sister, wary of cameras, wouldn't allow it.

"Hi, Mena," Lainey's dad said over the walkie-talkie. "Can you introduce yourself? I know we've met, and really good to see you again. But if you could just, you know, say who you are so Amelia can know you, too? Over."

Paranoid, suspicious. Amelia stood on the other side of the shore, her back to them, near enough to the walkie-talkie so she could hear but tensed up like she might bolt at any second.

Mena took the walkie-talkie. "Of course. I'm Mena, Kevin's daughter. Lainey's my stepmom. So good to meet you. Over."

"Thanks, Mena. So, the plan is for you two to be able to see each other, even though Lainey can't come to Louisiana and Amelia can't leave. And there's no reason why that can't happen here on these rocks where the water's fairly gentle."

The woman across the shore shook her head violently. Took a few steps away before their dad put out his arm to stop her. Static sounded through the walkie-talkie. Lainey wanted so badly not to be there, so badly. Mena's fingernails cut into the back of her hand.

"But of course, for that to happen, there need to be some ground rules."

Their dad kept pausing to listen to Amelia. "She's thinking that if I don't leave the shore . . . and, well, if you don't bring Mena, don't let Mena leave the shore . . . um, and the two of you don't go right away, wait until the sun comes over these trees, and the two of you don't talk when you're out there, then maybe it can work. Over."

The woman across the shore knelt down, her back still to the water, and cradled her head in her arms, the same way the little girl Lainey had grown up with used to do when she was stressed, overwhelmed. That little girl, who had always needed to give something up to allow for something else. No more pets so she could handle school. No more sleeping for a certain hour in the middle of the night and no more eating anything but the blandest foods so she could handle her piano lessons. Eventually, heartbreakingly, no more Lainey, or she wouldn't see a doctor and threatened to give up every single thing one by one until there was nothing left. They'd all pretended as long as they could that things were manageable, until pretending wasn't an option anymore.

"Lainey!" Mena was shaking her now. "Lainey, help her out. Come on."

Lainey picked up the walkie-talkie. "Hi, Amelia," she said and saw her sister raise her head at the sound of her voice. "That all sounds good to me. I'm also thinking that if I don't come out there until you have a chance to pick the best spot, and we don't wear shoes and don't let ourselves get too wet above the shoulders . . ." Amelia stood, turned sideways, brushed the hair back out of her face. "If we don't run away, don't shout, don't cry, don't react at all if the water's a little cold and don't mind if we see some fish, then we can sit on the rocks together quietly and I can put my arm around you while the water rushes over our laps. Over."

Lainey watched her sister and her dad talk for a moment, and then her dad hugged his younger daughter. "Sounds like we have a deal. When the sun's overhead, which should be in a little less than an hour. Also, Lainey, I'm getting married, and I wanted to tell you in person. And here we are, in person. But we'll talk on the phone in the next few days, and I'll tell you all about it. Over."

"Congrats, Dad. And happy birthday. Over and out."

Lainey and Mena poured some coffee from the thermos that Bertie had sent them off with while they waited for the sun to be in the proper spot for Lainey to walk out onto the rocks and into the river to meet her little sister. Lainey's dad was getting married to a woman she'd perhaps never meet. He was healthy, happy, but he wouldn't be around forever, and then what would happen?

Lainey spotted a lizard watching her. She crawled over to offer her hand, and it hopped right on and scurried to the front of her shirt. She also saw a piece of cloth, a scrunchie, that was packed into the dirt. She dug it up and held it out to Mena. Mena gave it a disgusted look and then said, "Awesome," and ran over to get her supplies to log it in.

"You want to tell me what's really going on with you?" Lainey said. "And I know it's not about whatever happened at law school."

Mena wrote in her notepad and tore out the page. "Yeah, some stuff went down in Brooklyn, with one of my roommates. It wasn't good." She looked up at Lainey. "Let's talk about it later. Over s'mores."

"Do you know what you're making yet?" Lainey asked.

She zipped the scrunchie and the piece of paper into a Ziploc. "I have some ideas. But it's way too early in the process to discuss it."

"Okay," Lainey said. "Just promise me that I can be there when you burn it down."

Babette Has Gone Missing

Becky Mandelbaum

I wanted to be alone, to have a break from my life, so I applied to an artist residency in the Southwest. I wasn't a writer but had, during a series of bored Sunday afternoons while my husband and sons watched European soccer, strung together enough sentences that a story accidentally formed. The sentences were about a woman named Babette who couldn't decide what to eat for lunch, so she began to eat her family, first their fingers, then their eyes. It was a disturbing, comedic tale of domestic life, or so wrote the judge who decided I was worthy of two months alone in New Mexico to produce more tales of Babette.

"You're doing what?" asked my husband, John.

"An artist residency."

"Since when are you an artist?"

"Since now, I guess."

"What if I woke up one day and told you I was running away to be a circus clown?"

"I'd be happy for you."

"Is that so?"

"Yes."

"Who's going to take care of the children?"

"I suppose you could."

He squinted at me. It was unusual for me to have something he didn't. Or perhaps he knew I had applied in part to get away from him.

I kissed my sons goodbye—they were thirteen and fifteen, still mostly animal—and reminded John what day the trash went out. Then I drove my 2012 Camry ten hours west, into the desert. I was happy to leave Kansas and its melodramatic winter. The whole state was like a premenstrual girl, moaning and crying one minute only to emerge clear-eyed and jubilant the next. I was sick of it. What I wanted was constant, reliable sunshine. I wanted a sky that was sure of itself, a sky that was cocky with light. A frat-boy winter.

I was to live alone in a casita that had once belonged to a famous photographer who had died in the bathroom from an aneurysm while straining on the toilet. Undoubtedly, the house was haunted, but the director could have put me in a dumpster and still I would have rejoiced, because the rotting banana peels and yellow-eyed rats would have been all mine.

In fact, the casita was cute, with adobe walls and a neatly made twin bed that spoke of solitude and uninterrupted sleep. No erections poking my back in the middle of the night. No morning breath, no icy toes.

The first thing I did was buy all the food I wanted, knowing nobody else would eat it. A whole cherry pie, a bag of those easy-peel clementines engineered for children, and so many candy bars the lady at checkout told me I was her role model. Then I went home, ate an entire sleeve of Keebler E.L. Fudge Elfwich cookies, and sat down to write.

What did writers do when they wrote? I imagined moody figures smoking cigarettes, twirling tumblers of whiskey as they bullied a typewriter. I didn't smoke or own a typewriter. What I had was Microsoft Word and an image of Babette—poor, rosy-cheeked Babette—digging a secret bunker beneath the suburban bungalow where she prepared bologna sandwiches and mended her children's clothes. I saw her carving away at the bunker while her family slept peacefully in bedrooms whose cleanliness she maintained. I saw her furnishing the bunker slowly, item by item, with the basic necessities of life—food, water, toilet paper, books. When the day finally came, she would take her cat, Perfect Cat Name, and descend into her bunker to live out the rest of her life in solitude. Every so often, she would emerge in the middle of the night, while her family slept. She would hover above their sleeping bodies, spritz her perfume on their clothes. In the morning, she would press her ear to the bunker's ceiling and wait for them to speak her name.

John called three times that first day. First to ask where we kept the AA batteries, second to ask whether we'd paid the gas bill, and third to ask whether New Mexico was beautiful.

"New Mexico is the most beautiful place I have ever been," I told him, and went on to describe the snow-dusted mountains, the sweeping mesas, the perfect cornflower sky. He grumbled something about radiation from nuclear testing, then hung up without saying he loved me.

To my great relief, day after day, the sentences arrived. Babette's story was there, like water in the walls. All I had to do was sit down and turn the faucet. It was as if I were not myself but rather a sink into which Babette poured words, and over time these words accumulated into paragraphs and then chapters—warm tubs in which I could finally, graciously submerge myself.

I had long found sanctuary in words, though never my own. When I was very young it was *Goodnight Moon*, the richly colored bedroom like opium for the eyes, the besmocked elder rabbit as soothing as God herself. Then it was Nancy Drew and *Lord of the Rings*. Then paperback thrillers in which the female protagonist always endured horrible suffering. Then discount romances, John clapping off the light midseduction, declaring it was time for sleep.

Like a baby who assumes, dumbfounded, that the language of adults is not for her, it had never occurred to me that I might be capable of writing, much less that I might enjoy it. Now, here it was, the joy. To think of the years I'd spent not writing was like looking directly into the sun. I kept doing it, in small bursts, to test the sensation of hurt.

By the end of my second week in New Mexico, John had called twenty-nine times and I had finished half a novel. Who knew I had half a novel in me? It was like waking up to find myself five months pregnant, the baby kicking mercilessly.

On day fifteen, I was making a ham-and-cheese sandwich when I heard a knock. I opened the door to a handsome man in a plaid wool jacket and beanie, a familiar wannabe-lumberjack type, not entirely dissimilar to John. "Hello," he said.

"Can I help you?"

"My name is Jameson. I'm the other resident."

I squeezed his outstretched hand. He had a ransom-letter grip, curt but demanding. "I didn't know there was another resident."

"There's always two," he said, insinuating that he had been here before, perhaps multiple times. I refused to ask, lest it initiate a longer conversation. I had begun to imagine my time in New Mexico as a pie cut into infinitesimally small slices. All day long, I could feel the pie getting smaller and smaller as my hunger grew greater. I wasn't sure what Jameson wanted but could already see his lips shimmering with hot purple filling. "I'm actually in the middle of a very important project," I said.

"Right, me too. That's why I'm here. I was thinking—what if we did dinners together, swapping every other day? That way we each cook less."

"You're offering to cook me dinner?"

"If you cook me dinner in return. An equal trade."

"I'm not Betty Crocker or anything." I was actually a very good cook, but I didn't want him to know.

"That makes two of us. I'll start tonight, and then you can go tomorrow. Meet at my casita at seven."

"Where is your casita?"

He pointed across a small field where crows normally gathered to scream at one another. From where we stood, I could see into his front window, which meant he could see into mine.

I worked until 6:55 in the evening. It was nice knowing somebody else would cook my food and do my dishes. When had anyone, other than the benevolent staff of Chili's, ever cooked my food or done my dishes?

Jameson's casita smelled like red meat and garlic. There was a bottle of merlot on the table and jazz music flowing from a portable speaker. I hated jazz music, but it seemed appropriate here, in this context, the way tomato juice is appropriate on an airplane. "Help yourself," Jameson said, gesturing to the bottle. He had a kitchen towel slung over his shoulder and was stirring a steaming pot.

While pouring myself a glass, I noticed his casita was much nicer than mine. The appliances were modern, and he had a dishwasher. When I peeked into his bedroom there was a queen-sized bed and an attached bathroom with a jetted tub. I wondered if the casitas were assigned at random or if accommodations were based on artistic merit.

"What type of artist are you?" I asked.

He kept his eyes on the pot. "I write plays."

"Anything I would have heard of?"

"Do you frequent New York?"

"I live in Kansas."

He smirked. "Then likely not."

I wondered who had given him permission to act so arrogant. Then I remembered how handsome he was.

"What about you?" he asked.

"I'm a writer."

"Anything I would have read?"

"I'm unpublished, actually."

He looked at me with new eyes, as if I'd told him I was a bewitched prairie dog disguised as a human female. "You must have submitted a hell of a writing sample. This is a highly competitive residency."

I blushed. I wanted him to continue praising my abilities, or to ask to read my writing sample, or to connect me with important literary people who could launch my career, but instead he said, "Will you please set the table?"

Setting the table was not part of the arrangement—I had planned to expend zero energy on his cooking nights—but I did as I was told, his compliment still swirling like a breeze under my skirt.

The meal was beef stew with potatoes and carrots. The meat was tender, gushing juice. "This is delicious," I said.

He blushed. "Maybe I'm half Betty Crocker." I felt, then, a sudden competitiveness and decided I would cook him a magnificent meal.

We drank the whole bottle of wine while talking about our lives. He was a big shot, friends with major producers and actors, one of whom I'd seen on an episode of *CSI*. He was working on a play about an elderly woman who falls in love with the teenage boy hired to bathe and feed her. "It's an erotic dramedy—there's lots of physical humor, as you can imagine."

"Sounds sexy. I'd see it."

"You would?"

"If I lived in New York."

"Well, maybe we can arrange a visit."

For a moment I stopped chewing, and a whole life bloomed before my eyes, the two of us hurrying down Broadway, he in a suit and tie, I in a gown the color of alpenglow. Where had this vision come from? It was still unfolding. He was looking at me under the marquee, fear writ bold in his eyes. "The critics will love it," I assured him. "And if they don't?" he asked. "Then we'll still have this," I said, gesturing to the empty space between us. Then he kissed me hard on the mouth, pulling away only to promise he would never clap off the light before I was done reading.

After the stew, Jameson produced two bowls of cold chocolate pudding. I adored chocolate pudding. Sometimes I made it for the boys, but John preferred complicated cakes, pies, and soufflés—anything that required hours of my time. Sitting across from Jameson, I carved away at the pudding carefully, as if it were made of glass. When my bowl was empty, I stood and told him thank you.

He walked me to the door and told me he'd see me tomorrow at seven. Then he put his mouth on my mouth and kissed me hard, with tongue, grabbing my ass like it was the face of a cliff and he a dangling mountaineer.

That night, I humped my pillow. Nobody had kissed me like that in years, John included. I used to love kissing. Boyfriends always told me I was good at it. Now, it sometimes disgusted me to see lovers kiss in movies. All that slobber, the soft tissue of the tongue. What kind of romantic activity was this, to taste the instrument with which another person tasted? Like clinking eyeballs or sniffing nostrils.

When I thought of John, of the wounded look he would give me if he ever found out about Jameson, I didn't care. I wanted more.

The next night, I stopped writing early in the afternoon, abandoning Babette midcrisis (her daughter, Allison, has just heard Perfect Cat Name meow beneath the floorboards). My goal was to produce a dinner even more delicious than Jameson's while maintaining an attitude twice as cavalier. At the store, I bought truffle oil, shiitake mushrooms, and a bottle of wine from the top shelf. Then I went home and put on the sexiest outfit I'd brought with me, a white jogging tank top and paisley midi skirt with a side slit. I dressed in front of the window that faced Jameson's casita. All day, I had lingered in front of this window—dressing and undressing, reading pages of my novel, a pen in my mouth, wearing pajama shorts and a bra. I imagined him at his window, watching me, begging to the clock to bring him closer to seven.

The risotto was fussy and required constant attention, like a baby. While stirring, I listened to an audiobook by a writer I admired who wrote bizarre stories and novels in which the women always turned lesbian, discarding their men in the same way one discards a used tampon, with relief and disgust, a touch of admiration for what has been endured. There was victory in her books. I once looked her up and discovered we were the exact same age, but she produced movies in LA and always looked like a baby doll come to life, her eyelashes splayed out like the heat waves of a tiny sun. I wondered if, one day, I might do something so notable she would look me up on the Internet and admire my photo. I, too, had great eyelashes and good hair.

The risotto was burning when Jameson sauntered in. Not even a knock. He took a seat at the table and poured himself a glass of wine. "I had a breakthrough today," he said, smiling to himself. "I think, if I play my cards right, this one could be Tony material."

"Isn't it strange," I said, "that so many awards are named for men—Oscar, Tony, Nobel."

"Tony is actually a nickname for Antoinette Perry—she was an actress."

I plated the risotto and brought our food to the table. "Then they should call them the Antoinette's."

"I'll propose the idea when I win one."

Was this flirting? If so, it seemed we were doing a tepid job. To heat things up, I took a bite of risotto and let a kernel of rice stick to the side of my lip. As soon as he looked up from his meal, I slowly wiped the side of my mouth with a finger, to draw attention to my tongue.

Alarm appeared on his face. "Did you cut yourself?"

My finger was bleeding. "Oh, shit," I said, wrapping my hand in my skirt. I hadn't used a knife since cutting the garlic—likely, there was blood in our food. I smiled, played it off. "Sometimes I get so swept up in my writing I don't notice things."

"Does that mean it was a productive day?"

"Very," I lied, squeezing my finger. "I, too, had a big breakthrough."

"Tell me about it."

I clenched the sphincter of my imagination and forced an idea. "The protagonist in my book, Babette—I've decided to let her succeed. To find love."

"What had you planned for her before?"

"She was going to abandon her family and live forever in a bunker. She was going to haunt her family until she died or they all moved out and forgot about her."

"And now?"

"Now a man—a handsome, worldly man she had always admired in her aboveground life—is going to accidentally dig a tunnel into her bunker. He and Babette will live out a beautiful, subterranean life with their cat, Perfect Cat Name."

"Why was the man digging a tunnel?"

"He was escaping from prison." I was proud of myself for churning out such great ideas on the fly. Here was the outline for the second half of my novel. Maybe I truly was a writer.

"What was his crime?"

"He was accused of murdering his wife, Babette's best friend, but he's innocent. His wife actually died by suicide, because she was secretly in love with Babette and Babette has gone missing."

"I like it," Jameson said. "I like it a lot." He was already refreshing his glass of wine. I worried he would be drunk before I was even buzzed. "However," he continued, his tone more severe, "you should know that a good writer never knows the ending of her story before she's gotten there. By charting out the whole plot of your book, you'll suck the story of its surprise."

"Oh," was all I could say. I squeezed my finger to assess the pain.

"As they say, no surprise for the writer, no surprise for the reader."

"Yes, I've heard that saying."

"They also say writing a book is like driving at night. You may only see as far as your headlights, but you'll get to where you're going."

"Yes, I've heard that one too."

He was looking not at me but at his glass of wine. "You'd be wise to follow the wisdom of other writers. We've been where you are before. We have information you don't."

"What if I just want to write the book I want to write?"

He smiled, as if I were a child who'd announced my plans to start a school for teddy bears. "You can write whatever you want—nobody's stopping you. But people will only read your work if it's good."

The risotto was overcooked and chewy, but Jameson devoured it with gusto, sucking his thumbs and wiping his plate with his bread. "I have a favor to ask," he said, scooping more rice onto his plate. "I'm in such a crunch with this play—there's a festival I'm trying to enter. I was wondering if you could cook dinner this week. Next week, once my deadline's passed, I can cook for you, all seven days."

I blinked at him, wondered what he looked like without a shirt.

"Okay," I said.

"You're an angel—I promise to make all your favorite meals."

There was a pause in which I wondered if he might kiss me or ask about my favorite meals. He did neither.

When it was time for him to go, I hovered near him, watched his fingers as he tied his shoes. He seemed like the type to wear leather loafers or fashionable sneakers, but he was wearing old hiking boots caked in mud. Some of the mud had crumbled onto my floor.

"Thanks for the company," I said.

"Thank *you*," he said, and then opened the door and left.

The next day, at sunrise, I stood naked in front of my window, turning one way and then the other. For dinner I prepared cheeseburgers and sweet potato fries, a favorite among John and the boys. Sometimes, on burger nights, John would ask me questions about my day and listen to my answers. I was excited to feed Jameson, but as soon as we sat down he sighed and removed the top half of his bun, set it aside.

"Are you watching your carbs?" I asked.

He smiled as if I'd asked him something silly and also slightly embarrassing, like where babies come from. "I'm sensitive about my bun-to-patty ratio."

After the meal, before he could tie his shoes, I put a hand on his arm. It was hairy and muscular, exactly like John's. He looked up at me, his eyes brimming with pity, and I braced myself for rejection. Instead, he stepped closer, placed a hand on my breast and squeezed. My brain made the sound *honk, honk*. He came toward me all the way and stuck his tongue in my mouth, pressed his crotch into my crotch. My whole body whirred and wheeled.

Then he stepped away, wished me a good night, and left.

Things went on like this. Night three was black bean enchiladas and topless grinding, my breasts bouncing in his face. Night four was pesto grilled cheese and handsy play. Nights five and six were tuna noodle casserole, a dish I normally made when I felt like disappointing my children, followed by more handsy play. I wanted all the way in, but Jameson was holding back.

"Is it because I'm married?" I asked one night as he was lacing his boot at my door, more dirt crumbling onto the linoleum.

"It's because we have weeks ahead of us. We should pace ourselves."

"Weeks won't be enough."

He glanced up at me. "They'll be enough."

On the seventh and final night, I prepared a dish I'd been making my whole life, a meal born of sexual frustration and laziness. My mother had taught me how to make it, and her mother had taught her, going all the way back to the days when women prepared meals around fires. It was peanut butter and jelly. As a side dish, I bought a bag of Lay's and put a handful on Jameson's plate. He eyed the sandwich, his frown so hyperbolic it was like a child's drawing of a very sad man.

"I can remove the crust and cut it diagonal," I said, "but only if you stay the night."

He looked morosely at his plate, then at me. "Okay."

When his sandwich was gone, he put his plate next to the sink. Then he walked toward me and unbuttoned my jeans with a workaday coolness, as if opening a box of cereal. Once I was naked he seemed to wake up, his tongue everywhere at once, his eyes heavy and wet.

The sex was average but seemed to bring Jameson great joy, which made it a little better than average for me in the end. I liked knowing I'd done well. He wanted to talk after, which was strange, because John never wanted to talk. I was very tired—I had slept poorly all week—but tried to stay awake as he told me about the play he'd submitted to the festival, how alive it made him feel, like he had just climbed a mountain and was waiting for a hot air balloon to take him away into the clouds. Success is what he meant by the clouds. All this time, while he was working on his play, I had been rotating in front of the window like a rotisserie chicken or ransacking the thrift store down the street for a secondhand negligee that didn't smell of divorce.

I was pleased when he broke his monologue to kiss my shoulder, the way John used to when we were younger, before we had the boys. He whispered in my ear. "Tell me more about Babette."

"You want to know?"

"Yes."

Carefully, in my best sexy whisper, I trotted out the details of Babette's marriage, her home life, her decision to dig the bunker. I told him about Perfect Cat Name and the way Babette danced around the beds of her sleeping children. The deeper I went, the larger my affection for Babette grew. I loved her, and I wanted other people to love her too. I wanted readers to find her brave, likable, sexy, and smart. I wanted young girls to hang Babette posters on their walls, dress as Babette for Halloween. I wanted her to be famous the way Harry Potter and Batman were famous. I wanted to become CEO of the Babette Corporation and live forever off the fruits of our labor.

Eventually I stopped talking or Jameson stopped listening and we fell asleep, still attached, my breath on his neck, visions of Babette blooming and fading behind my eyes. At some point we adjusted so that I was big spoon—for some reason, even though I was much smaller than both John and Jameson, I always ended up big spoon. When I woke it was still dark out and Jameson was getting dressed. I could hear the click of his belt buckle.

"Where are you going?"

"You were snoring."

"Really?"

"Like a tractor." Then he pecked me on the cheek and was gone.

Nearly twenty years of marriage, and John had never once told me I snored.

The next night, I knocked on Jameson's door, eager to claim my portion of the trade. My plan was to be persnickety, to demand he cut my steak, refill my wineglass, pepper my salad. When he didn't answer, I knocked harder. Maybe his jazz was too loud, but I couldn't hear any music. Maybe he was in the shower, but he shouldn't have been in the shower, he should have been cooking my meal, preparing for my arrival. That's when I noticed the lights in the kitchen were off, that his car was not in the little carport behind the house.

I went home, drank a glass of wine, and watched his house through my window. An hour passed, then two. I was starving but refused to eat until he fed me.

I went to bed without dinner. When I woke, I was hungry and furious. I went outside to see if he had returned, but his car was still gone. That's when I noticed a note taped to his door. I hadn't seen it last night, in the dark—it was taped very high on the doorframe, where I could only reach if I stood on tiptoes. Was it arrogance or laziness to leave the note on his door and not mine?

On the outside of the envelope was my name. I tore it open and found a letter. *The best thing happened*, the letter read. *A very famous movie producer has invited me to visit his chalet in the Swiss Alps. He wants to discuss a screenplay I sent him—did I mention I was also writing a movie? Thank you for the dinners. Perhaps we'll meet again.—Jameson*

I crumpled the letter, threw it into the grass, and kicked the front door, which swung open—he hadn't even locked it. I wondered if the director of the residency, an elderly man named Lester St. Peters who seemed not at all concerned with how we used our time in the casitas, even knew that Jameson had departed.

I called out, "Hello?" When no answer came, I let myself inside. His casita, without him in it, seemed even larger. The kitchen was cheerful, sunlight gushing in from the large window above the counter. He had left behind several objects, as if he only had so much time to arrive at the chalet before the producer revoked his invitation. There was a bar of Irish Spring in the shower, almond milk in the refrigerator. A stack of printer paper and a bouquet of red pens. On his counter, a container of molasses cookies I'd given him days before.

That evening, I tried to write—the last chapters were mapped out in my mind, all I needed was to put my fingers to the keyboard—but no words appeared. I missed Jameson, or maybe the sensation of looking forward to Jameson, or maybe the sensation of waiting for Jameson to acknowledge my talent and pull me up to his level of glory. There was a pit in my stomach, not unlike the one I had carried with me throughout my marriage, and which I had planned to fill with writing.

For dinner, I ate cashews and toast. When I tried to sleep, I couldn't sleep. The injustice of it all consumed me. Jameson had arrived here, in this beautiful town with its snow-dusted mountains, had written a play and a screenplay, and was now off eating soft cheeses with important men who would soon give him armloads of money in exchange for his writing.

Meanwhile, I had six voicemails from my sons and John, saying they loved and missed me. The messages enraged me. I did not want to be loved and missed. Not yet. What I wanted was to finish my book, to impress myself and the people around me. To prove to John, and myself, that I was more than the life I'd led so far. I wanted him and my sons to read my book and think, *How blind we must have been not to see that, all this time, while folding our jeans and buttering our pancakes, our quiet, milquetoast mother was cultivating a rich inner life.*

I stopped tossing in my bed and sat up, clicked on the lamp.

Quietly, I put on my coat, my pants, my shoes. I crept from the house and crossed the empty field to Jameson's casita, my laptop and a bottle of white wine in tow. Then I posted up at Jameson's desk and began to work. A new energy filled me—anger with a touch of envy and misery. He had tried to distract me, to trick me into believing it was love I needed instead of my own victory, my own hot air balloon into the clouds. I imagined standing on the mountaintop, ejecting an arrow into the fabric of his stupid playwriting balloon. Whether I had the strength to pull back an arrow in real life, I had no idea, but this was my brain, my imagination, and I could do whatever I wanted.

There was still food in his pantry—some cheese crackers, a jar of lentils, the stale molasses cookies. I ate it all. I used his soap, his shampoo, his towels. I wrote and wrote and wrote, finishing the final chapters as if releasing the last sneeze in a series of several good-feeling sneezes. I was done.

When I returned home, John and my sons were teary-eyed with relief. They had baked me a carrot cake and cleaned the house so thoroughly that their fingertips were pink and raw. John gave me roses, and my sons hugged me with such force I worried I might pee. I was touched and felt a pulse of guilt at the sheen in John's eyes—he'd truly missed me. I wondered, for the first time, if there was a pit in his stomach that I was responsible for filling.

They asked me questions about the residency, and I answered the ones I wanted to. I told them about my novel, which I had put in a folder on my desktop and planned to return to in a month's time for revisions. Jameson had mentioned that all great writers put their work away for a minimum of thirty days so they could revisit it with fresh eyes.

"Did you do everything you wanted to do?" John asked.

"Yes," I answered. "I believe I did."

He squeezed my hand and nodded. "Good. I'm glad you got it out of your system."

I nodded, unsure what he meant. Did he think writing was an object I needed to pass or a temporary illness, like a flu, that would eventually burn out? I couldn't explain that the novel had become my system, the organ through which everything else now circulated. My dream was to publish it and acquire money with which to write another novel, and another, and as many as I could before I died.

What happened next is that a breaker flipped. Life returned to normal. I cooked dinner, cleaned messes I had not made. I drove my sons to their friends' houses and did everyone's laundry. The old resentment bubbled up through the sewer grates in my heart, but this time all I had to do was remember the novel, and the toxic waste would retreat back to the subterranean bog from which it arrived.

When the month was over, I woke in a cheerful mood, as if a dear friend was set to arrive from out of town. I put on a nice outfit, sat at the kitchen table, and opened my laptop, a machine I had mostly ignored since returning from the residency. I checked the desktop, eager to read the book's first sentence, to see if it still held the same intoxicating energy it had in New Mexico. But the document wasn't there. Panic overtook my body, coursing through me like an injection of ice water. I clicked around, frantically opening every folder, searching the history on Microsoft Word. It was gone, as if I'd never written it. Hadn't I written it?

"Where is it?" I asked my family. They were in the living room, watching a WWE smackdown fight. One half-naked man was slamming another half-naked man with a metal folding chair.

My sons didn't answer—they had no idea what I was talking about.

"Where's what?" John asked, muting the TV and turning to look at me. I scanned his face but found only his usual blank stare.

"Nothing," I said. "Never mind."

I took a shower, telling myself I could cry as hard as I liked for the duration of the shower. After, I would not allow myself to think of the novel, or Babette, or the hot air balloon in the clouds. I would not chastise myself for failing to save the book to a flash drive, like any sensible person would have done. I would move on, pretend none of it had ever happened.

The shower was quick, more of a rinse. When I got out, I looked in the mirror and remembered how nice a body I had, my breasts full, my thighs strong. Despite all my years of cleaning with toxic chemicals, even my hands looked young.

Three years later, long after I'd given up hope that my laptop might spontaneously regurgitate my book, John and I were in the living room, watching television, when an advertisement for a movie came on. The trailer opened to a shot of a beautiful woman, played by Scarlett Johansen, listening to her husband drone on about the stock market while she washed dishes. In the background, a swarm of towheaded children wreaked general havoc on the house. The next scene cut to her in a garden, digging around with a trowel. She's suddenly struck by an idea—the voiceover even says, *Suddenly, she's struck by an idea*—and the next thing you see is Scarlett outside, under cover of darkness, with a shovel. Next scene, she's in a tastefully decorated subterranean lair, arranging her things, when a trickle of dirt begins to crumble from the wall behind her. Suddenly a finger pokes through, and eventually a man emerges. It's Timothée Chalamet—a little young for Scarlett, you're supposed to think, but it's part of the appeal. Cut to them making love, fingernails raking down backs. Cut to Scarlett at night, dancing around her sleeping family, head thrown back in silent laughter. Cut to Scarlett cradling her cat, Perfect Cat Name, hushing its meows as her beautiful daughter, played by an anonymous young actress certain to rocket to fame, puts her ear to the kitchen floor. *Coming this Christmas*, boomed the voiceover, *to a theater near you*.

Then it was over. My skin sizzled as if I had become the television screen and the television screen had become me.

"Now that," John said, patting my knee, "looks like a stupid movie."

Contributors' Notes

Lauren Acampora is the author of *The Hundred Waters*, *The Paper Wasp*, and *The Wonder Garden*, all published by Grove Atlantic. *The Wonder Garden*, a debut collection of linked stories of which "Swarm" is a part, won the GLCA New Writers Award, was a finalist for the New England Book Award, and was longlisted for the Story Prize. Her first novel, *The Paper Wasp*, was longlisted for the Center for Fiction's First Novel Prize, and her second novel, *The Hundred Waters*, was chosen as one of *Vogue*'s Best Books of 2022. She was named a 2021 NYSCA/NYFA Artist Fellow in Fiction from the New York Foundation for the Arts. Lauren lives in Westchester County, New York, with her husband, artist Thomas Doyle, and their daughter.

Elizabeth Altomonte's stories have appeared in *Image*, *Inkwell*, *The Kenyon Review*, and the *Missouri Review*. When she is not writing, she is a quiltivist and assemblage artist. Elizabeth lives in Florida with her husband and an adorable Bernedoodle named Lady Wildflower.

Therese Eiben worked in book and magazine publishing for decades. She received her master's in creative writing from Brown University. Recent publishing credits include "Oscar Kilo: We Are All Not OK" (*Evergreen Review*, 2022) and "Pass the Baby" (*december magazine*, 2018). She lives in Hudson, New York, with her husband and their merry cocker-pit mix, Charlie Parker.

Ernest J. Finney writes stories and novels, mostly set in California, often in the San Francisco Bay Area, where he grew up, and in the Central Valley and Sierras. His short fiction has been included in several anthologies, among them *O. Henry Prize Stories* and *Best*

American Mystery Stories. His books include four novels, *Winterchill, Lady with the Alligator Purse, Words of My Roaring*, and *California Time*, and three story collections: *Birds Landing, Flights in the Heavenlies*, and *Sequoia Gardens: Stories of California.* His novella *Elevation: 6,040* won the California Book Award in Fiction in 2016.

Catherine Gammon's most recent novel is *The Martyrs, The Lovers*, and her new collection, *The Gunman and the Carnival*, is forthcoming from Baobab Press. Her previous novels are *China Blue, Sorrow*, and *Isabel Out of the Rain.* Her work has received support from the NEA, NYFA, the Fine Arts Work Center in Provincetown, and the Virginia Center for the Creative Arts, among others, and has appeared in literary magazines for many years. Before beginning residential Zen training in California in 2001, she taught at the University of Pittsburgh. She lives again in Pittsburgh with her garden and her cat.

Laura Venita Green is a writer and translator with an MFA from Columbia University, where she was an undergraduate teaching fellow. Her fiction won the 2021 Story Foundation Prize and appears in the *Missouri Review, Story, Joyland, Fatal Flaw*, and translated to Italian in *Spazinclusi.* Her translations appear in *World Literature Today* and the *Apple Valley Review.* Originally from Louisiana, she lives with her husband in New York City.

Kerry Hardie's eighth collection, *Where Now Begins*, was published in 2020. Her seventh, *The Zebra Stood in the Night*, was shortlisted for the Irish Times Award. She has won many prizes, including the Michael Hartnett Award, a Patrick and Katherine Kavanagh Award, the Suspended Sentence Award, the Laurence O'Shaughnessy Award, the IOTA chapbook award, and the Irish National Poetry Prize. She has written two novels: *A Winter Marriage* and *The Bird Woman.* Her work has been widely translated and has been much anthologized in Ireland, the US, and the UK. She lives in Kilkenny with her husband Seán and is a member of Aosdána.

Gabrielle Hovendon's writing has appeared in the *Georgia Review*, *Gettysburg Review*, *Cincinnati Review*, *Southwest Review*, *Electric Literature*, *Verse*, *Boulevard*, and *Ninth Letter*. She has an MFA from Bowling Green State University and a PhD from the University of Georgia. She lives in Los Angeles, where she is currently at work on a collection of hybrid works about queer identity and a novel about protest and revenge set in a family stonecutting empire in nineteenth-century France.

Becky Mandelbaum is the author of the novel *The Bright Side Sanctuary for Animals* and the story collection *Bad Kansas*, which received the Flannery O'Connor Award for Short Fiction, the 2018 High Plains Book Award for First Book, and was a Kansas Notable Book. Her work has appeared in *One Story*, the *Sun*, the *Georgia Review*, *McSweeney's Internet Tendency*, and elsewhere. Her writing has received support from the Helene Wurlitzer Foundation, Writing by Writers, and Lighthouse Works. Originally from Kansas, she currently lives in Bellingham, Washington.

Frank Montesonti is the author of two full-length collections of poetry—*Blight, Blight, Blight, Ray of Hope* (winner of the 2011 Barrow Street Book Prize) and the book of erasure, *Hope Tree (How to Prune Fruit Trees)* by Black Lawrence Press. His poems and stories have appeared in several literary magazines, including *Tin House*, *AQR*, *Black Warrior Review*, *Poet Lore*, and the *Missouri Review*. He lives north of Joshua Tree, California, and teaches creative writing and composition at National University.

M. G. Stephens is the author of twenty-nine books, including such recent works as the novels *King Ezra*, about the poet Ezra

Pound, and *Kid Coole,* a boxing novel, both published by Spuyten Duyvil in 2022. He also published the hybrid work of fiction and poetry *History of the Theatre or the Glass Fashion* (MadHat Press, 2021), about an out-of-work actor who lands the part of Hamlet. In 2023, he is to publish a book of stories, *Jesus' Dog,* and a short collection of poetry, *Ornithology.*